Fire and Ice

The Fall Begins

Nathan Young

To order additional copies of this book, contact:
Xlibris Corporation
0-800-644-6988
www.xlibrispublishing.co.uk
Orders@xlibrispublishing.co.uk
302936

Fire and Ice

Contents

This book is dedicated first of all to those people that I have had the immense privilege to get to know over the years. Without whom, I have no idea where I would be right now. So Stacey, Lucy and especially Rocky . . . this is for you.

This is also dedicated to everyone in Havant, and of course Leigh Park, and I am truly proud to be able to say that this little town is the place where I grew up.

Prologue

The Fall of a Good Man

Have you ever just wanted to quit and stick your head in the sand somewhere?

I have. I used to be a normal man, with a life, and with a home of my own. Not anymore. I wanted out and I wanted it over.

I used to keep telling myself that I wasn't a killer, but I never really believed that. I don't live for the kill, nor do I go looking for trouble. Trouble always had an irritating talent for finding me after all.

There was only one course of action left open to me now; and that was to finish this game once and for all.

The bullets whizzed past me as I ran and I knew that Carter was right behind me. My own weapon, freezing cold and heavy in my hands was ready to fire. I only needed one shot. I wouldn't miss my chance.

Cumbria, 27/07/2011. 5.56pm

I t was a warm and humid day, well above the norm for the time of year. The sun was sat high in the sky, sinking almost lazily into the West as if to say *no! I'll hang about and roast you all for another couple of hours.*

To the south, coal black storm clouds were beginning to form as a result of the week's heat wave. It was as though nature was oblivious to the fallout and the devastation that had taken place several hundred miles away on the south coast of England just half a day previously.

For Danny Patterson however, it felt like no time at all as he stared silently at the concrete complex half a mile east of his position. His cold blue-grey eyes remained fixed as the last of his initial fear drained from his body, only to be replaced by an unyielding and steely determination that had been his constant companion for the past five years.

Just half a decade ago, Danny had been a normal man, a normal human who dreamed of a quiet life; a wife he adored, and kids he loved with a job he was proud of, something he now knew to be a mere pipe dream. It was a bitter pill to swallow for him and an ever present nightmare that plagued his every move and his every thought time and time again.

Danny hadn't wanted any of it; not from the moment the first bullet flew past his ear to the death sentence that hung over him now like his own personal cartoon storm cloud.

The air felt strange, as though electrically charged by whatever lay between him and the only thing that had kept him in the fight for so long. The only thing he had left to fight for.

Danny's thoughts turned back to the beginning; back to a time when life had been simple. He saw the deaths of his best friends once again, saw them dying in front of his very eyes and feeling that all-too-familiar sensation of being pounded in the gut by the grief and the anger that briefly consumed him.

It had taken several years to fully learn mastery of his emotions, but like a drug it had changed him, right down to the very core. He was no longer the quiet, respectful young man that his friends had known, changing instead to a cold, merciless and instinctive killer perfectly adapted to the life that came hand in hand working for the SIS and MI5.

Of course, it hadn't been his choice. After everything that had happened, after everything that he had been through, it seemed ironic that he had lost everything that had been so dear to him on the day he would die, for he was facing his final battle, soon to become just another soldier in an unmarked grave.

What would once have defeated him back in the beginning now had no effect, the anger, and the paralyzing grief ebbing away now as he reined it in swiftly, stuffing it out like a used cigarette and retaking control of his emotions. Danny took his eyes off his target after ten minutes, slipping his left hand into his jacket and removing the Browning Hi-Power from its shoulder holster. He inspected it inch by inch, popping the magazine from its housing at the butt of the gun, checking the bullets and slipping it back it with a soft click as the magazine slotted flush into its housing. He thumbed back the hammer, and flicked the safety to make it ready for firing. He treated the weapon as though it was an old friend, showing it a great amount of care and respect. It had been plenty faithful to him these past years, never once failing him in combat. Danny pulled the thick silencer barrel from his pocket, fixing it to his weapon swiftly and expertly and stowing it down on the passenger seat.

The sound of an oncoming vehicle behind Danny alerted him to its presence, and he hunkered down as the white Land Rover came closer. It was perfect for dealing with the rough terrain. It was a well built and beautifully designed vehicle that was robust yet capable in many different uses.

The idea clicked in nice and quickly, and Danny picked up the Browning from the passenger seat of his outdated Ford Mondeo as he clambered out of the car. Playing it cool he flagged down the driver, who pulled up alongside him looking slightly confused. Danny looked into the car curiously, noticing immediately the SA-80A1 assault rifle on the back seat. The driver was certainly a merc, Danny noted to himself, the short cut hair and outdated British Army fatigues instantly gave him away to anyone with a trained eye.

"You alright mate?" the driver grunted in a slow, almost drawling northern accent.

"Not really, I got myself lost and my car broke down, any chance you could help me?" Danny replied in a rich Scottish accent that would have sounded real to anybody south of the border. The merc in the land rover regarded him with suspicion and hesitated; Danny pressed his advantage. "Please, man I was meant to be in Gretna three hours ago, I'm sure the car jus' needs a jumpstart."

The merc clambered out of his Land Rover with a bit of a grumble, and quietly followed Danny back the few metre's to the Mondeo. He leaned inside and popped the bonnet.

"What's your name?" Danny asked brightly, as he walked back to stand by the side of the car.

"Pete," was the gruff reply, "and yourself?"

"My name's William, William Wallace," Danny smiled.

"Look, man I can explain to your commanding officer that you were just helping me out if you need?"

"No thanks, I won't need you to do that." Pete replied quietly.

"Aw come on man I insist, its only right," Danny replied a little more forcefully.

Pete was visibly irritated by Danny now, straightening up and glaring at him.

"Look, I don't want . . ." he began angrily, but Danny cut him off right away, his face giving away no emotion as he brought the weapon up.

"You know Pete, you're right to be pissed off," Danny told him, dropping the accent and reverting back to his normal voice. "I just wanted you to know, I don't have any regrets."

Danny flicked off the safety catch, and before Pete could even so much as blink, he squeezed the trigger. The Browning kicked back in his hand as it expelled a single 9mm parabellum round square into Pete's forehead. The silencer did its job well, muffling the sound nicely as the merc's head exploded into oblivion. The body hit the ground as Danny flicked the safety back on and stowed the weapon back in its holster.

Crouching down, he searched the body at his feet, retrieving the ID badge before dragging the body back to the boot of the Mondeo and hoisting it in there unceremoniously. Danny slammed the boot shut and glanced around just to make sure that he wasn't being watched. Satisfied that he was alone, Danny strode sharply back to the Land Rover and flung himself into the driver's seat.

Reaching behind him, he grabbed the rifle, checking the magazine and putting it on the passenger's seat instead.

The SA-80A1 was the standard issue assault rifle and light support weapon of the British Army. Manufactured jointly between BAE systems and Heckler & Koch, it entered service in 1987. It had an effective range of 450 metre's when fired with an aperture iron sight whilst later variants of the rifle were kitted out with telescopic SUSAT sights. Gas operated and using a rotating bolt mechanism, the SA-80 fired the 5.56 x 45 mm NATO cartridge from a 30-round detachable STANAG magazine and had a fully automatic rate of fire of between 610-775 rounds per minute. Danny was familiar with the weapon, having used it a number of times in the past. He remembered how he had been unable to fire it from his left hand because of the ejector port and cocking mechanism being located on the right side of the receiver, and that in turn made aimed fire from the left hand impossible. *What a pain that had been.*

Danny drove on towards the checkpoint, keeping the speed down to thirty to avoid any unwanted attention. He began thinking again, thinking about the long, hard and deadly chain of event that had led to this moment. The final battle was certainly upon him now, there was no escaping it and there was no putting it off. If Danny was to die; if that was what his destiny was, then so be it. In his heart he instinctively knew that he wouldn't just roll over and take it . . . he would fight, just as he always had. That was the reason he has survived this long. Danny eyed the checkpoint ahead; it was nothing more than a small observation booth, but as he had expected, it was manned and guarded by half a dozen mercenaries. He slowed to a crawl and wound both windows down as the first guard walked towards him. He stopped the car and reached for the ID badge in his pocket as the merc looked in from the passenger side.

"You're not one of our guys, who are you?"

Damn it, Danny told himself as he lifted his hand back out of his pocket, *So much for the element of surprise.*

"New guy, sent down from Aberdeen" he muttered quickly, affecting the Scottish accent again.

"First we've heard of it, I was under the impression Aberdeen's crew were all dead," the guard replied.

"Few of us got out in time, hold on . . . got them orders here somewhere." Danny began to pat himself down, keeping the act up until he slipped his hand into his jacket whilst the guard at the window looked away. He grabbed his weapon from the back of his trousers, flicking off the safety once again as he kept his eyes on the merc. The guard spun, obviously recognizing the soft *click* of the safety button being depressed and began to react, bringing his rifle up. Danny was the quickest, aiming and firing twice. Both bullets slammed into the skull of the guard and the body collapsed as the head exploded into a cloud of blood and brain matter. The remaining guards came at him now, and Danny took cover as they opened fire, getting down flat across both seats as the bullets rained down on the car. Bits of fluff and glass from the seats and windscreen pelted him as he covered his face. The hailstorm of rounds ceased almost as quickly as it had begun and Danny thanked god for escaping with just a few cuts from the glass. Forgetting the rifle, he sprung up and threw himself through the windscreen, sliding across the bonnet and sprinting for cover behind the reinforced concrete booth as the hailstorm of lead resumed. He settled into the weaver firing stance and waited patiently. The lull came as the first rifle fell silent and Danny turned, opening fire.

The first two guards dropped as the rounds hit them, whilst the survivors scattered. They attempted to take cover and flank him. Danny was too quick, leaving cover and taking out the guard moving to his left. Spinning round as the other two disappeared round the opposite corner of the booth, he moved back, cutting them off and killing the fourth with another burst of fire. the final guard made to open fire as Danny emerged into the open and he threw the gun at him in desperation, and it hit the target square in the face, disrupting his aim just enough. Danny tackled him just before he could recover, sending the both of them sprawling to the ground. The fistfight was short, but fierce. When Danny slowly rose from the ground moments later, he looked down at his enemy. Picking up the discarded SA-80, he steadied himself. The gunshot issued noisily for miles around, and after a moments thought, Danny turned on his heel to face the larger complex and with a sigh, he went to meet his fate.

1. In The Beginning

I was happy to be the man I was, and no words could ever describe just how happy and satisfied I really was with my life. I had somehow managed to survive the trials and tribulations that came hand in hand with being from Leigh Park, and even after all this time I still love that place regardless of what had happened.

They say that good things come to those who wait; well I had done more than enough waiting in my time and maybe, just maybe the happiness I was finally beginning to experience was my reward for what we had gone through over the years. But as always with life, it always found a way to destroy you in the end, and I had been so sure that I would spot the threat looming before me in time to avoid it, or even prepare for it.

I still can't believe how quickly the fall began . . .

Southern England, 01/04/2006

N ight fell like a curtain over the south coast of England. The stars began to blink into existence as the sky darkened and the moon rose over the hills and above the trees.

Soon enough the supporters of the local football team began to make their presence known, singing their way through the streets on their traditional route towards the stadium. It was part of the life blood of the town, its pride and joy. In the town centre partygoers and people enjoying a night out in the pubs made the town more alive, even though most of them would be nursing a hangover the next day whilst working at the same time. This was Havant.

The ancient town had lay on the border between Hampshire and West Sussex since records began, growing from a small roman settlement and into the bustling town is was today. Like all towns and cities and like all countries of the world she had her own stories to tell.

The gig ended just after nine, with the band receiving a standing ovation from the fans who had packed out the tiny community centre.

Danny Patterson applauded the fans alongside his friends on stage and was still in a state of disbelief that even after two years doing what he loved in a band that he loved even more, the two hundred-or-so fans crammed into the tiny hall in front of them could make so much noise. It overwhelmed him as he bid them a safe trip and a good night. After a while they left the stage, ducking back into the even smaller play gym. The band was a mixture of emotions, ranging from the exhausted and tired to absolute delight.

Danny was the first to make his way across the room to the tiny tea area in the corner, sticking the kettle on and grabbing a cup from the cupboard. He stood there, leaning against the worktop as he listened to the rest of the group chattering away.

Steve, the lead singer was the loudest, the born worrier that he was, worrying that the demo tape they had put together hadn't been sent in time.

Danny wasn't a particularly rowdy man, always preferring to be on the edge of things instead of being caught up in the middle of it. He had a full complement of thick black hair that was cropped short and curved around the shape of his forehead. His physique was one of a tall, muscular man who took good care of his body and who was physically fit. His eyes were a cool blue-grey in colour and looked almost as though they were cold and calculating to the usual passer-by. He was twenty years old, and the only son of a soldier who had died in combat when he was a toddler.

He had been the driving force in the formation of the band, now known as *Common Purpose*.

All five of them had discovered a talent for music after a trip to watch the local football side play in a local derby away from home. Steve and Bill had both discovered a natural talent for singing on the train across, Jack and Ade were both already known to be very good with bass and guitars, and Danny himself had taken a snare drum to help ramp up the atmosphere and had proved to be a good drummer. It was then that *Common Purpose* had been born.

"Relax you old git, I sent it earlier," Danny called quickly as Steve continuously fretted away

"What did you say?" Steve snapped back quickly, not catching what Danny had said.

Danny turned, looking innocent and trying to hide a snigger. He shrugged his shoulders theatrically. "I didn't say anything."

"You bloody well did."

"You need to turn your hearing aid up mate. Your age is starting to catch up with you"

Bill, Ade and Jack all exploded with laughter as Steve went red with embarrassment.

It took a few minutes for the laughter to subside before Danny carried on. "I sent the damn demo earlier Steve. Chill out."

"Thank god for that," Steve answered with a sigh of relief.

Danny turned away again as his mobile went off in the depths of his sports bag. He began ploughing through it in attempt to answer the call in time but failed miserably. He smiled again as he recognised the callers number displayed on the screen and hit the redial button.

The band had been together for two and a half years now, getting together whilst in their first year at college.

Steve; the oldest of the band at twenty two years of age, had been moved around a lot as a youngster due to his parents splitting up and divorcing and had picked up a sight cockney accent from a prolonged stay with relatives in the east end of London from the age of seven. Returning home to Havant with his younger brother aged nineteen, He had first met Danny and Bill at a football match and they had hit it off instantly. Joining a college course together, the three of them had soon become the best of friends.

Bill on the other hand was different. Aged twenty one and born in Strathclyde, Scotland. His parents had decided to relocate to the south of England prior to his birth. He kept a part of his accent due to his parents continued use and a strict understanding of his country's long and proud heritage ensued to this day. He was powerfully built, albeit short and a little stocky and had a head of sandy hair that he took a great amount of pride in gelling every day.

Ade was the youngest member at nineteen years of age and was relatively well known across the area. His sense of adventure and good looks set him apart from the rest of the band and had earned him the attention of a number of their female fans in recent months. He had a fiery temper, but he had never shown it whilst doing a gig with the band and nevertheless Ade Collins was a loyal, honest person who commanded the respect of every last one of his friends, relatives and admirers. Tall and gangling, he towered over the likes of Steve and Jack, who both seemed quite diminutive for their respective ages.

Jack Harper however was again different and at twenty years of age he had the darkest past of them all and as a kid he had been drawn into the dark world of gangs and street warfare.

He finally escaped his former life aged seventeen when he was hit by a car that had been stolen by a local thief. It was then that he had decided to rebuild his life and had been introduced to the others by Steve not long after.

It took a minute for the call to connect as Steve roared with delight on hearing that the local side had won their match.

Hello?

The voice was female, and was one that Danny knew only too well. The sound of her voice, kind and full of life sent a shiver down his spine.

"Hello Stacy," he murmured. "You called?"

Yeah hun, how'd it go?

"It went really well, I think," Danny chuckled. "You missed a belter . . ."

The line cut out and Danny quickly hit the redial button before being alerted to the fact that the other four were staring silently over his shoulder towards the French doors at the end of the room. He looked around slowly, and beamed.

Stacy was stood to the left of the doors, her long brunette hair tied back in a long ponytail whilst her fringe waved slightly in the spring breeze. She smiled and waved timidly before striding quickly across the room and threw herself into his waiting arms.

"I didn't miss it. You were fantastic tonight," she told him as she leaned up to kiss him. Danny held her in a vice tight grip as she pulled back to look into his eyes.

Stacy Ryan had been romantically involved with Danny for the past three years. She was a beautiful woman who attracted practically everyone who met her, mostly as a result of her chocolate brown hair that seemed to shine ever so slightly in the light and a pair of warm hazel eyes that sparkled with life. At nineteen years of age she was well known across the area and very popular.

"I never saw you out there. Where were you?" Danny replied with a smile as they swayed on the spot.

"At the back where I could keep an eye on your female admirers," she replied darkly. "Hi guys," she added hastily to the others with a smile.

Danny blushed slightly and let her go.

"I don't see why you need to be worried Stace. You and I both know that they were probably checking out Ade *as usual*," said Steve sarcastically.

Ade swore at him in return, his voice sounded muffled by the door that led to the little tea area in the corner. Steve grinned like a Cheshire cat on steroids whilst Stacy fought back a laugh.

"I guess so," she grinned as she took an empty seat, "but I've got to watch my man eh?"

Danny smiled again and continued to pack his stuff.

"I thought it was Danny's job to watch *his* girl, not the other way around?" Ade guffawed from the kitchen.

Danny shook his head at the bad joke. He felt that there was no need for insinuations over things he had done over three years ago, but he also knew that Ade, being the joker of the group, would never let him live it down.

"Who scored for the Hawks tonight?" he asked Steve as he reached out to wrap his arm around Stacy's shoulder.

"Yeah, it is about time *somebody* scored around here," Ade muttered in a somewhat allusive voice as he left the kitchen.

Whilst sudden fits of laughter tore through Bill and Jack, Steve put his head in his hands and groaned as Danny retracted his arm from around Stacy's collarbone and sprang, chasing Ade around the room to a rich peel of laughter as Stacy watched them. A few moments latter Ade was in a dishevelled heap on the floor begging for mercy and frantically apologising as Danny playfully attacked him. Danny released him soon after, helping him up and laughing with him as they threw their arms around each other's shoulders and strode back to the group.

*　　*　　*

The mobile rang for the third time and the driver grew tired of ignoring it.

Pulling onto the verge he switched the engine off and answered the call.

"What?" The tone of his voice was angry, a tone of irritation at the disturbance.

Are you there yet? The voice was cold in comparison, sharp and unforgiving.

"I'd get into the estate a lot quicker if you weren't distracting me so much."

You want to remember your place, there's a lot more people who'd kill for the job you've been given. I could easily pull you out, Carter.

Carter paused quietly, engrossed deeply in his thoughts.

"As if I need reminding," he hissed in reply. "Just let me get on with my job and I'll be in touch when it's done."

Good.

The line went dead and Carter threw his phone back on to the passenger seat with a grunt of frustration.

Opening the glove compartment, he removed the Beretta 9mm pistol and the magazine and inspected both quickly and quietly, before slipping the magazine into the chamber and releasing the safety catch. Carter slipped the weapon into the inside breast pocket of his trench coat and adjusted his tie.

He was a professional mercenary, a gun for hire who offered his services to the highest bidder no matter whom or what they were. He was in his late thirties now, an ex SIS officer who saw service in Iraq and in Afghanistan as a soldier before being discharged dishonourably in the aftermath of a mission-gone-wrong in the months leading up to the first Gulf War.

He was a cold, efficient killer, no longer caring what happened as long as the job was completed. He checked the time and the details of what this particular job entailed once again and switched on the engine of his 4x4 and it roared into life. Under the bonnet was a twin cam, 16 cylinder Vee8 diesel engine with an idling speed of 1200 RPM. Revving the engine to maximum, Carter turned off the verge and with a flurry of speed continued into the estate.

*   *   *

It wasn't until well after ten that Danny, Stacy and Bill left the venue, stepping into the cold night and joining the last few stragglers from the gig and from the football a few streets away. Heading up into the massive council estate that was Leigh Park, they chatted away happily about the night's events.

On many street corners they passed varied groups of teenagers, most of whom ignored the trio. Some however jeered at them and wolf whistled Stacy at times. Aside from that the council estate was silent, a strange side-step from the reputation that many held as gospel truth.

It was a well-known fact that Leigh Park was one of the largest council estates in the United Kingdom. One of the most deprived areas in Europe; the council estate had been built as an overspill suburb in the aftermath of the Second World War and had steadily descended into a state of near-lawlessness before an improvement in the early noughties. The gangs that had sprung up alongside it rose and fell like ancient civilisations until only six of the biggest remained. Those early gangs ensured Leigh Park's devastating reputation following a series of violent underground street wars with the gangs of Eastleigh and Crawley, the last of which had been fought in the spring of 1990. Since that dramatic period a tentative peace had held between the three, and the "new guard" refused to break the peace again. Those lessons had been learned from the past, although the bitterness and hatred held firm on the football terraces in isolated pockets.

The trio turned into a narrow alley as they made their way into The Warren; the topmost part of Leigh Park, hurrying though the darkness. Stacy felt the cold creeping up on her and drew closer to Danny for warmth. He responded, putting his arm around her waist and held her tightly.

"I've wanted to experiment with the drums for a while," Bill said after a few minutes silence. "I think we should try incorporating it more next time."

"Yeah, but to be realistic how are we going to sort that out? You're not that good with your timing and it's going to take a while just getting it right," Danny replied.

Bill laughed. "Aye mate that's true but it's worth a go at any rate."

"We're going to be in for the bloody long haul then. You honestly up for months of rehearsing to get it right?"

Bill shot Danny that trademark look of stubbornness that had so defined him throughout the years the two had known each other. Danny quickly withered and accepted defeat.

"Right then, about this demo you sent?" Bill continued after a moment's silence.

"We sent it to all the local radio stations, Solent, Express, the Quay, Galaxy, the lot," Stacy replied.

"What songs?"

That caused Danny to think quickly. "Three of our anthems, that one with some of the Hawks fans in it and two of those emotional buggers that set your mum off that time."

Bill blushed as he remembered that time. They had been performing in the club house of the local side, Havant & Waterlooville when it had happened; over a year ago when they had only just seriously started out as a band. Bill and Steve had belted their hearts out in a number called *Remember* and just as they hit the chorus his mum had descended into tears and had to be comforted by Bill's dad. Bill had been informed about it by an observant Danny after the gig had ended. It had been an event that embarrassed him but made him more certain about the future they had as a band.

"Christ, imagine what she'll be like if we make it big," Bill groaned. "It doesn't bear thinking about."

Danny merely smiled.

*   *   *

2. War and Peace

What is happiness? Is it an emotion you feel or is it the sense that everything is right as rain. I wasn't sure I knew that myself. I was happy, my life was perfect and I would have been a fool to wish for more. It's funny, because fate has a real knack for destroying everything.

They say that when good men go to war, even they have rules. They were wrong, and I was as far from being a good man as I could get.

C arter pulled onto the kerb and switched the ignition off once more. He was certain this road was the place as he scanned the immediate surroundings, noting the gang of teenagers on the street corner to his right and the density of the houses on both sides of the street only confirmed his suspicions.

He checked his weapon once more, setting it down on the passenger seat and located the targets picture and accompanying details. He studied both once more, taking his time to fully memorise the face in front of him.

A young face is was too, that was Carter's first thought. He had hardly any hair where it had been cut so short, but relatively good looking nonetheless, with brown eyes that would no doubt melt most girls' hearts.

A shame he has to die, Carter told himself. Returning to the paper the details were on, he noted the name and age of his target with a smile. He was a guitarist in a local band hoping to make it big, only 20.

"Jack Harper," Carter murmured quietly.

*   *   *

"No way Danny," Bill chortled. "Last time you did that at Eastleigh we were nearly kicked out."

"Lighten up, it's a derby. That's what we're supposed to do," Danny laughed as he gave Bill a playful shove. "Check out that jeep over there, you don't tend to see one of those in such a good condition around here."

Bill whistled in admiration.

"Very nice, someone around here must be doing well."

Danny nodded in agreement as they were alerted to the sound of a car horn behind them. Turning to face the oncoming car, they recognised it instantly as Jack's little Fiesta as it pulled up alongside them. Steve was in the passenger seat and Ade was in the back, and the three jumped out quickly, all wearing identical masks of shock and awe.

"Just heard that express are giving some of our songs a bit of air time within the next ten minutes," Steve said in a triumphant voice, "Looking for you three was like looking for a very small pin in a very big haystack."

To say Steve was exited was a true understatement. He was completely ecstatic.

"This is Leigh Park you daft git, what were you expecting, a cosy little trip around Hayling?" Ade grinned as he strode over to hi-five Stacy.

Danny's eyes went wide with surprise, along with Bill, who looked close to fainting.

"You're joshing me?" he replied, "Seriously Steve you're having me on aren't you?"

Steve stood there and gaped at Danny with disbelief written across his face.

"Mother of god," Bill moaned in a weak voice as he clicked on himself.

Danny beamed wildly for a moment and then went completely crazy, mobbing Steve as though he had just single-handedly won the World cup and letting out a triumphant roar of delight as the others bounded into the fray. Stacy stepped back as she giggled at the carnage the lads were creating and began clapping along to them as they continued to make a nuisance of themselves.

All around them curious neighbours stared out of their windows in various states of slight bemusement; some of whom were less than happy at having their evenings interrupted by a group of merry teenagers.

They soon calmed down however, as they wanted to be ready for their big moment on the airwaves. Danny took Stacy's hand, pulled her in close and kissed her full on the mouth as Jack jumped back into his car, turning the ignition so that only the electrics ran. Booting the stereo to life, Jack tuned it quickly into Express FM just in the nick of time as the DJ began a long winded speech on new talent and how more had been discovered.

"Guys, quickly!" he gestured and they piled around him as he turned up the volume.

> . . . *earlier tonight before the show began, my producer informed me of a slight change in schedule. Our normal feature has been postponed for the moment following something very interesting that came to our attention here at Express FM. As most of my regular listeners know I am a great advocate for the emergence of new talent within the*

*music scene, and it would appear that there are others here
that share this view. This morning we received a demo from an
unsigned band in Leigh Park called Common Purpose . . .*

"This is it lads," Steve whispered quietly. His reward was a quick
smack in the head from Danny as the DJ continued his broadcast.

*. . . have decided to play two tracks from this band for you
now, please send in your views on the usual number and
e-mail address. This is the first track, a real rock anthem
that has captured our imagination. This is left handed.*

As the fast beat of the song began streaming across the airwaves
and Bills voice began belting out the lyrics, they began singing
along, turning the volume up fully. For the lads things could get no
better. They were one step closer to achieving their dream.

*   *   *

Carter heard the sound of the oncoming car on the opposite
side of the road and ducked down slightly as it pulled up and came
to a halt beside the three youngsters he had noticed just moments
previously. Instantly he had begun watching them discreetly for
any indication of his targets presence. The girl was dismissed
instantly, followed quickly by the lad whose arms she was in and
their friend. His frustration began to grow once more as he then
began to survey the trio of lads who had just climbed out of the car.
The streetlamp right next to them instantly threw their faces into
relief. He noted the one who was on the pavement first, instantly
dismissing his ginger hair before moving onto the next lad, soon
dismissing him too as a sudden roar of delight echoed across the
street and pandemonium broke out amongst the group of lads as
they celebrated something. They eventually calmed down and as
the final lad strode around to the driver's side of the vehicle a pang
of recognition hit Carter; everything from his short hair to his facial
features, all the same.

He had found his target.

*   *   *

The song ended with a flourish and Jack switched off the radio. They were amazed at what they had just heard; shocked even.

"I need a drink," he groaned and clambered out of the car once more. The others followed suit, gathering around the bonnet quietly. Danny pulled Stacy close once again and held her. Nobody spoke for a while as they recovered from the shock. They had heard their best work live on radio, broadcast across the south coast. They were almost famous and one step closer to achieving their dream.

"It's amazing, were doing it, here and now. We're living the dream," Bill murmured after a while.

"Brilliant," was the quiet reply from Steve.

They had spent two long years working towards this very moment. It was their crowning glory and it was their prize. They had hoped and prayed for years that it would happen and nothing could describe how they felt as that tiny moment of success slowly dawned upon them. Things couldn't get any better for Danny and the other members of common purpose.

*   *   *

Carter flicked the send button on his mobile phone, sending a two-worded text message to his employer:

Target acquired.

Within minutes he received the reply he was hoping for and checked the chamber on his weapon one last time. When he was satisfied with his inspection he pocketed it again, before slipping all his information on the target into the glove compartment for safekeeping until he could destroy it efficiently. He checked his tie in the rear view mirror and opened the door and climbed out of the 4x4.

*   *   *

They had spread out a little more as the chatter began to change into what they would do as rock stars. Bill had moved towards the street lamp near to Danny and Stacy, who were cuddling silently a few metres from the others. Steve, Ade and Jack remained leaning on the bonnet of the car.

Bill noticed the smartly dressed figure in black striding across the road towards them first, pointing him out to the group.

"A businessman making house calls at this time? Come on it's getting on a bit isn't it?"

"Bill that does happen here as well as the rest of the country mate," Steve chuckled.

All eyes were fixed on him as he came to a halt a few yards away from them, standing in the road as he gazed towards Jack and Steve.

"You lost mate?" Jack piped up.

"Jack Harper?" the dark figure asked in a sharp, crisp voice.

Jack hesitated for a moment, doing a double take between himself and Bill.

"Yeah, that's me," he responded slowly. "Who are you?"

Carter moved forward into the light and smiled.

Jacks eyes went wide with horror as Carter brought his pistol to bear on him, stumbling backwards onto the pavement and falling to the ground. Carter's weapon followed him down as Bill stood rooted to the spot with fear; Danny automatically pushed Stacy behind him, shielding her with his body as he sensed the danger. Something snapped in Danny's mind, kicking him onto autopilot and he began to react as the first shot rang out into the night.

Without hesitating or thinking, Steve had thrown himself into the line of fire. The bullet hit him in the left shoulder, followed swiftly by a second that hit him in the centre of the chest. He corkscrewed in mid-air as it exited the other side, ripping a golf ball sized chunk of bloody flesh from him. Danny pulled Stacy down behind the car as the next two shots rang out and he could only look on in horror as he saw Steve hit the ground.

He moved quickly, diving across the bonnet and onto his feet as Carter spun to face him. Danny was too fast and slammed into him with so much force that it threw Carter clean off his feet.

They crashed down into the road in a tangle of limbs and began wrestling furiously. Carter's weapon went spinning off across the road as Danny attacked repeatedly, landing blows again and again as Carter struggled to repel him.

Ade screamed for help repeatedly as Steve lay face down in a growing pool of blood. Jack began to panic as he attempted to stem the flow from the three gunshot wounds Steve had sustained. The blood loss quickly became uncontrollable as Ade attempted to help somewhat vainly. People began trickling from their homes to see what had happened after hearing their calls for help as Danny and Carter continued to battle it out in the road.

Carter managed to throw Danny off him and stumbled to his feet. Danny sprung up quickly to continue the confrontation and they came to blows again. Raging forward, Danny lunged at him. Carter dodged the attack nimbly and counter attacked. The first blow caught Danny square in the midriff, knocking him off balance as he doubled over. Carter struck again as Danny straightened up, this time catching him in the temple. He hit the ground, rolling with the punch.

Danny felt dazed as he clambered to his feet. Out of the corner of his eye he saw Stacy, screaming hysterically, calling his name. He felt her fear numbing his own, saw the others desperately attempting to save Steve, surrounded by others, all bound together in a common cause. Something deep inside him drove him onwards still, that tribal instinct that spurred him forward in the defence of his friends.

Carter stretched his arm out and reached for the discarded weapon that lay in the gutter as Danny launched himself at him once more. He brought him down again, and he lost his grip on the weapon as he returned his attentions towards Danny.

Danny stood over him, a look of hatred on his blood-stained face as he glared down at Carter.

He returned the stare, his gaze piercing through Danny's eyes with a look of pure hatred. He was completely fearless.

He laughed, infuriating Danny even more, glanced over at Steve's motionless body on the pavement as the sound of sirens filled the air, racing towards them. He Smirked as Stacy sprinted towards them suddenly; it wasn't missed by Danny, who looked up sharply.

"NO! Go back! GO BACK!" he roared desperately, but she didn't falter. Carter seized his chance, striking out with his foot as Danny turned to the side. The blow caught him sharply in the back of the leg and he buckled, hitting the ground with a gasp of pain.

Carter sprang to his feet with his weapon in hand, aiming at Stacy first, who froze a few yards from Danny, then at Danny himself as he scrambled to his feet. They both stood stock still, staring at the weapon Carter held in his hands.

"Leave her alone," Danny growled. "She's not part of this."

"Danny . . ." Stacy began in a frightened voice.

Tears streamed down her face as she looked between Danny, Carter and the gun in his hands. Her arms were stretched almost halfway towards Danny's body as she froze, and in that moment she was more scared than she had ever been before. This time even Danny couldn't stop it.

"Well isn't that sweet? You've done yourself well there," Carter purred smugly as he kept the weapon trained on Danny. "In all these years I've never killed a couple as young as you two."

Stacy's eyes widened with shock. "No . . . please!" she begged.

"Who are you? WHY DID YOU DO THIS?" Danny bellowed.

"Leave the girl alone and take me if you really have to!"

"You should not have intervened in affairs that don't concern you," Carter replied in a smooth voice, "I'm a reasonable man so no, I won't kill the girl. You on the other hand, I really should."

Carter steadied his aim, directing the weapon very precisely towards Danny's forehead. Danny steadied himself too, looking Carter firmly in the eye as he waited for the bullet to put him out of his misery.

It didn't come.

Carter lowered his weapon, returning the stare confidently.

Stacy rushed into Danny's arms and breathed a sigh of relief as Carter spoke once again.

"It's not my place to kill you just yet. Your fate will be decided by The Rogues soon enough. I can promise you that."

Danny glared furiously at him, too angry for words as Carter turned away and began striding towards his car.

"You still haven't answered my question . . . who are you?" Danny barked after a moment.

Carter came to a halt and looked around at him once more.
"My name is Carter."

"Well I promise you *Carter*, your time will come. Sooner rather than later," Danny growled. "Remember my face; it's the last thing you'll ever see."

Carter merely chuckled, jumped into his car and sped away.

3. Grief, Anger and Revenge

Anger was all I knew, hatred was all I could feel. I had always sworn that I would never be like the rest of them; that I would lead a calm, peaceful life. Get married and start a family. There was a time when I could see that, but now all I could see was a long dark tunnel ahead of me, with no end and no daylight in sight.

S tacy pressed herself against Danny's body, finding comfort and warmth in arms. Her fear subsided slowly as he pulled her closer to him and held her tightly.

"You okay?" Danny murmured.

"I'm scared Danny," she replied shakily, "who was that man, why did he . . . ?"

She couldn't bring herself to say the words. The mere thought of seeing one of her best friends so brutally attacked scared the very essence of life from her. For all she knew, it could have been her.

"I don't know, but I'm going to find out."

Danny felt groggy as he spoke. The fight had taken a severe toll on him and he suspected that the strike to the temple he'd received was the root of it as they stumbled back towards the crowd surrounding Steve and the others. Danny picked his way through the crowd, emerging to see Ade and Bill attempting to save Steve's life. Jack had stood back, unable to carry on. He was shaking uncontrollably as Danny stumbled towards him.

"Is he okay?" Danny groaned quietly.

Jack couldn't speak for shock, managing just a slow shake of the head.

"I think . . ." he eventually stuttered, "I think we're losing him. It's my fault Danny."

Stacy joined Danny at his side as he began to feel dizzier. He felt the world spinning as his sight dimmed, and even the sirens that filled the air seemed distant and drawn out. His sight blurred as his head throbbed painfully. It felt like it was about to burst.

The pain took over completely as the adrenaline wore off and everything went black as he collapsed, with Stacy's agonising screams etched into his ears.

* * *

Carter's 4x4 sped out of the estate and onto the motorway. Inside he was smirking, happy at his work. He had worked up an appetite and decided to get himself a takeaway from a very good local Indian he knew a few miles down the road. Carter sent a quick message to his boss informing him that Harper was not dead, but another was. He knew it would have the effect The Rogues wanted one way or another, and Eastleigh wanted the blood of their rivals badly enough to accept any death on enemy land, however it all depended on whether both sides played ball.

Harper wasn't that important, Carter told himself, not to be a threat to The Rogues anyway. The name had been randomly picked, it could have been any one of them; even the girl.

He was confident that his boss would be satisfied enough to pay up. His mobile beeped once, indicating a reply. Carter checked it at once and smiled. It was just as he had hoped; His employers had accepted the kill he had made. Fairfax would be happy; things were proceeding in the direction they wanted. The battle lines were being drawn.

But even then, something was bothering him and for a fleeting moment, he had honestly believed that Colin Patterson was still alive. Was it possible that that had been the son he had once seen pictures of back in the unit?

He shuddered as he returned his attention the road in front of him.

*   *   *

Things began getting lighter; Danny's eyelids fluttered open and shut continually in a disorientated fashion, giving him only faint glimpses of the hospital room he was in. As his sight returned he looked around, becoming conscious of his surroundings in the small dark hospital room, and of the figures surrounding him. On his immediate left, Stacy was at his side. He smiled weakly as he felt her hand squeeze his own slightly. Ade was right next to her, he was covered in blood, albeit Steve's blood.

He looked straight at him, unable to register any emotion. On Danny's right, Bill was consoling Jack, the both of them also covered in blood.

"What happened?" Danny groaned drowsily. His head continued to pound like a never-ending drumbeat.

"You took an almighty smack to the head," Ade replied in the same restrained tone. "We . . . no she thought you were dying when you hit the deck. Even the paramedics reckoned you were lucky to be alive."

The sides of Danny's mouth twitched slightly as he fought back the grin that was building slowly.

"How's Steve?" He murmured as he turned his head slowly toward Stacy.

Her face fell as fresh tears began to descend down her cheeks as she clutched his hand tighter. She couldn't bring herself to say it.

Danny stared in disbelief, looking repeatedly between Stacy to Ade.

"Please . . . please no!" he begged of them. His face fell with grief at once, fell with desperation. "Tell me he's not dead . . . Stacy?"

She looked up at him slowly as he took hold of her hands and squeezed them gently.

"Is Steve okay?" Danny asked again, quieter this time.

He awakened instantly from his drowsy stupor, lurching upright. She shook her head, unable to speak through her grief and in the end it was Ade who put him out of his misery.

"Steve died on the way in", he murmured, "took a bullet to the chest. It entered around half an inch from his heart and it severed the pulmonary as it went through."

Danny welled up, tears spilling across his already blood-stained face and the grief and the shock took him for its own as he broke down. The anger came first, building up deep within and exploding into life as he roared out Carter's name and. The disbelief and the hatred came next, building into a crescendo as he began to struggle to his feet.

Stacy rocked back, terrified by Danny's deepening anger whilst Ade lurched forwards to calm him down and restrain him.

"Danny, DANNY!" Ade growled as he struggled to pin him down. "DAMN IT DANNY, THIS WON'T BRING HIM BACK!"

He glared at him, eyes wild with grief and rage and struggling against Ade's hold only infuriated him further. In the corner of the room Stacy had slipped into hysterical sobs; Bill rushed to her side in an attempt to comfort her.

Danny gazed at her almost instinctively; seeing her that way crushed his heart and he began to calm himself. His breathing became drawn out and even, and Ade responded by loosening his hold on him.

"Just what the hell do you expect to achieve by kicking off and running after this Carter bloke eh, Danny?" Ade demanded.

"Revenge, Ade," Danny muttered quietly, not meeting his glare as he spoke. He couldn't face it. Instead, he concentrated on keeping calm, blocking out the grief. "That bastard took Steve's life, so why not take his? An eye for an eye"

"I know, but he was Eastleigh. Do you know what that'll mean when the Elite find out? If you . . . if we attack on their land?"

Danny raised his eyebrows, turning intently to meet Ade's gaze for the first time. "They attacked us, on *our* land!"

Ade hesitated as he digested the fact, "You are *not* a killer, Danny."

"Am I not?" Danny growled.

"Enough!"

Danny and Ade looked up at Jack as he rose from his chair sharply. He eyed them all tensely and strode straight towards Danny, "Danny's right. We could easily destroy them, but they are just as capable of pulling a real number on us. Steve is dead because of me. It's my fault, so if anyone's going to do the killing, it *will* be me!"

Danny opened his mouth to reply furiously but Jack silenced him with one look.

"Damn it Danny, you've scared her three times tonight already!" he growled, pointing at Stacy's dishevelled figure in the corner clutching at Bill for support.

"First you attack that armed psycho, nearly getting the both of you killed in the process; secondly you end up in here with god knows what whilst she drives herself insane thinking you're dead!

"And thirdly," he glared at him sharply, "you want to just run into enemy territory and risk a war just to get even? Answer me this; do you have a bloody death wish or something? How the hell do you think I feel?"

Danny dropped his gaze as remorse washed across him. He knew Jack was right about it all.

It's suicide, he told himself.

The feeling of remorse washed deeper within him as he calmed down slowly, building a barrier against the grief that urged unchecked throughout his body. He stared at Stacy, a nervous wreck before his eyes. It had always hurt him to see her upset, even from the night they had met. He switched his gaze to Bill, who returned the gaze solemnly and a feeling of understanding passed between them.

"Ade, let me up please," he murmured quietly.

Ade hesitated. "You calm?"

Danny nodded, although Ade was not entirely convinced. He released his hold on Danny, who immediately sprang up to remove the IV from his arm.

Although his strength was returning, Danny was still a little unsteady on his feet as he crossed the small floor space to where Stacy was sat. Bill nudged her slightly as he approached and as she looked up, her face trembled once more. Rising swiftly, she began to sob again as Danny surged quickly forwards to wrap her tightly in his arms; she returned the embrace almost violently as he kissed the top of her head.

"I'm so sorry Stacy, truly I am," Danny murmured as he pulled her tighter.

"Are you okay?" she sniffed.

Danny kissed her again as he freed one hand to pull her face up to look him in the eyes. "Yeah, yeah I'm fine."

"Why did he kill Steve?" Stacy asked as Danny stared down into to her eyes. He couldn't answer as his eyes glazed over and he fought back tears of his own. Stacy clung to him as though her life depended on it.

They remained in their tight embrace for what seemed like hours and were finally interrupted by the young female nurse who had bustled into the room to check on Danny. Taken by surprise at his recovery, she quickly ducked back out of the room. Danny stared after her with a brief look of confusion. His intuition quickly flickered and he quickly withdrew from the embrace to move to the door to his right where the nurse had just disappeared. He edged the door open slightly in order to see into the hospital corridor and spotted the luminous yellow jackets of the two police officers who were waiting impassively by the ward reception desk. They started towards the nurse that had just left the room and proceeded to speak to her quietly.

"Bloody hell," he moaned as he slipped the door shut and sloped back to the bed, Stacy followed quietly and wrapped her arms securely around Danny as he leaned against the bed. His arms quickly wound around Stacy in response, locking her slender body against his own.

"Danny?" Bill piped up, "What's just got you in a knot?"

"Cops," he grimaced in reply. Danny hated police, along with all authority.

Bill rolled his eyes; his thoughts shared Danny's sentiments as he took his turn to have a peek through the door at the officers. They started towards the door and Bill cursed as he snapped he door shut.

"Great, this is about to turn into a bloody soap opera."

He skulked back to his chair as a soft knock on the door greeted them. The nurse popped her head inside the door once more somewhat timidly.

"Mr Patterson? There are a couple of police officers here who would like to talk about what happened to you and your friends. Would you like to speak to them?"

Danny looked up slowly as a spasm of grief struck him, his throat tightened with the memory so fresh in his mind. Unable to speak, he merely nodded. The nurse disappeared and half a second later the door swung swiftly open to reveal the two officers. They entered and shut the door behind them. Danny eyed them meaningfully. Beneath the luminous jackets both officers were wearing trouser suits, giving them a slightly ridiculous appearance; the taller of the duo wore what seemed to be a simple brown suit that wouldn't have given him too much protection from the cold. The same could also be said of the officer who stood just behind him, hence the need for the luminous coats. It gave Danny the fleeting impression that they were auditioning for some amateur production of *Joseph and the Amazing Technicolor Dreamcoat*.

"Danny Patterson?" the officer on the left asked. "I'm DCI Greene and this is DC Stewart, we want to ask you a few questions about the events of tonight, if we could."

Danny kept his eyes on the two officers, saying nothing as they showed him their ID. David Greene was the taller of the duo, stern looking and in his forties; his piercing blue eyes were easily diverted by Danny's own.

Alex Stewart was the complete opposite, youthful and slightly timid, his face showed sympathy towards Danny and everyone in the room.

"Steve was a friend of yours?" Greene asked.

Danny inclined his head in acknowledgement once again.

"Could you describe the events leading up to the assault on Steve?"

For the first time, Danny averted his eyes as the grief came back with a vengeance and tore at his emotions like a hurricane. Slowly, he reined it in once more, unable to speak.

"Don't you think it's a bit soon?" Ade cut in angrily with a glare towards Greene.

Greene and Stewart both looked at him with an expression of shock.

"Sir, we are sympathetic towards you all. What you went through is too much for any man or woman, let alone kids like yourselves.

"However you must understand that we have a duty to find your friends killer before he kills anyone else," Greene replied quietly.

The room descended into quiet as Ade and Greene shot angry glares towards each other.

Danny relinquished his hold on Stacy and moved towards the window, leaning heavily against the frame and staring out over the sprawling city of Portsmouth in the distance, he worked himself slowly into a state of calm, making sure of his emotions with a struggle.

"We were just standing there. It happened in the blink of an eye," he muttered after a few minutes of quiet and shifted his position to put his back to the window. "The radio was playing one of our songs and we were pretty happy about it as you'd imagine.

"Then Bill spotted that guy walking across the road and the next thing I know he's pointed a gun at Jack."

"Do you know why?" Stewart asked.

It was the first rule of the streets that you never stitch up anyone to the police, no matter who they were or what they had done. Danny didn't care about rules however. If Carter could play dirty then so would he.

"I don't want to talk about it anymore, please respect that. I need some time . . ."

Danny was set in his course. As soon as the hospital released him Carter would be made to pay for what he had done . . .

"Of course, we'll need you to come down to the station to help us with our enquiries. We want to catch this guy and put him in the nick where he belongs," Stewart replied with an encouraging smile.

Danny moved slowly towards Stewart, extending his hand.

"If you need me to, then yes, thank you DC Stewart."

Stewart accepted the handshake warmly, clasping Danny's hand and giving it a single quick jerk.

"Once again, I'm sorry for your loss."

Danny watched Greene follow Stewart out the door before turning back to the others.

"What now?"

"I don't know," replied Bill with a grimace.

*   *   *

Greene shut the door to Danny's room and stepped into line with Stewart.

"What do you think?" he asked Stewart quietly.

"I think it's going to turn nasty. If I was one of them, I'd be looking for revenge and I'd be willing to bet that's what they'll do," he replied quietly. As much as Greene refused to believe it, he knew Stewart was right. *Happy little punk*, Greene told himself, the lad was down with the kids.

"We'll need to keep an eye on them then; this guy obviously doesn't know what he's potentially stirred up."

Stewart smiled slightly as they headed towards the stairs.

*   *   *

Carter pulled off the road onto a private dirt track just east of the town of Fareham, it streaked in a perfect line straight towards an old barn. Overgrown hedges flanked the road the majority of the way.

The barn had remained devoid of all use for several years before now, until Carter had commandeered it with his small private army of mercenaries the previous week. They had continued to set up all the gear that had been sent to them in his absence, including enough weapons and ammunition to fight a small battle. Carter brought the car to a standstill outside the barn, switching off the engine and gathering all of his gear. He climbed out of the car and walked into the makeshift command centre that was Tithe barn. Two sentries stood sentinel outside, respectfully snapping to attention in a well drilled fashion as he passed by them.

The main barn area was a hive of activity, dotted around were tables of maps and communications gear of various types. A huge tactical map of the local area lay across half the length of the far wall. It could have been a World War Two command post.

John Harcourt stood in front of the large map, studying it with his back to Carter. A tall, powerfully built man, Harcourt was in his late forties and aging gracefully. His chocolate brown hair had a tinge of grey to it and was receding slightly. He was Carter's right hand man and second in command of the operation they were running.

All for the greater good of the United Kingdom, he would tell himself sometimes.

Carter dumped his stuff and moved to join him swiftly. Harcourt turned slightly to acknowledge his Commander.

"You look a bit rough; did he put up a fight?" He boomed in his upper class accent.

Carter eyed him meaningfully and smiled. "Something like that, Fairfax wasn't wrong about that lot in Havant."

"So it's done?"

"Yes, it's done. I doubt it'll take too long to complete our objective."

Carter fell silent as he turned back to face the map. His jaw set hard as he lost himself, deep in thought whilst he stared at one area in particular.

Harcourt noticed the silence after a moment, frowning slightly as he realised how unusual it was.

"Carter, old chap, you sure you're okay? You seem a little . . . quiet?"

"I'm fine, just thinking about something."

Carter shrugged the thoughts off as he spoke and began to move off toward a basic little tea area on the far left hand side. Harcourt followed him.

"What about the setup, John? Is the cell ready?" Carter asked quietly as they walked.

"Twenty lads on site right now, with weaponry and ammunition to see us through should the military discover our location," Harcourt rolled off before pausing slightly.

As ex-soldiers none of their number were entirely happy about the idea of killing their brothers and sisters who formed the armed services that they loved so dearly; Harcourt all the more so. However, they all accepted that it might be a necessary step towards completing their objectives. Composing himself as they arrived at the tea area, he continued.

"There's another twenty sitting in reserve dotted around the area, just in case.

"Obviously we've begun our part of the destabilisation plan with the strike on Havant, so all we need to do for the moment is sit back and let them make the next move."

Carter nodded in agreement as he poured himself and Harcourt a cup of tea.

"Has there been any news from the other cells?"

"The best, everybody's been calling in to command over the last few hours. They're all set up and ready, even the sleeper agents are ready," replied Harcourt as he accepted the cup of tea from Carter.

Good news, Carter told himself as he took a sip of his tea.

Even then, they couldn't afford any slip-ups, but there was still that kid. It was a real blast from the past for him. Danny Patterson was the dead ringer of an old friend of his . . .

Carter shook the thought from his mind once again before he settled back into the silence of his thoughts.

*　　*　　*

The Police station at Havant was one of those old dilapidated concrete jungle type monstrosities that looked from the outside to be in urgent need of repair. The only thing that identified it was an old blue lantern that hung over the front entrance to the station itself.

Greene and Stewart arrived back in the ancient car park at the rear of the station in their Skoda Octavia just after two in the morning and the freezing conditions outside began to take hold almost immediately as Stewart switched off the engine. Jumping quickly out of the car, they hurried into the warmth of the station.

Originally due to finish their shifts at 10pm, they had been forced to overrun due to what was on paper a Gangland hit. That was Greene's mentality as they settled down in the cramped staff area to compile their paperwork on the night's events.

As Stewart sat at his desk, one thought in particular began to creep into his mind. His intuition began to flicker that things might not be that simple. It was too kind and too easy, Stewart thought to himself as he began to think things through for the first time. What would honestly call for such a violent reaction towards a bunch of seemingly innocent friends? Of course there was an instant answer that popped immediately into his brain: Eastleigh.

Alex shook his head in disgust as he recalled the briefings from previous years from the super as they returned to the front of his mind. As a local boy himself, he had heard all of the old stories that shot around the town like some obscene game of Chinese Whispers. For a long time he had still believed that was exactly what they were, until he had joined the service. That was when he discovered that some of the stories were actually rooted in some aspect of truth. It certainly made sense as well, because let's face it; who else would actually be *that* stupid?

But then again there was something troubling him. He knew that Eastleigh didn't just walk up to you, ask your name and then try to kill you. Both sides didn't care *who* you were. You were the enemy by right of being there. It was always a case of kill-first-ask-questions-later, not the other way around. He shook his head with disbelief as he went over his desk to write up his report.

4. The Fall Begins

The time dragged slowly, whilst the grief refused to abate. I look back on those days with nothing but horror and disbelief. I never would have realised that those days would signal the beginning of the end and by the time I had realised what I would potentially become, it was too late.

My battle was beginning and there was only one place this dark path was going to lead me.
The fall begins . . .

Day One

Tick Tock goes the clock, and what game shall they play? Tick Tock goes the clock, now summer's gone away?

Day Two

Tick Tock goes the clock, and what then shall he be? Tick Tock until the day that thou shalt die for me.

Day Three

Tick Tock goes the clock, and all the years they fly. Tick Tock and now it's time; the fall begins today.

Day Four

Tick Tock goes the clock; he chose his path and lost her. Tick Tock goes the clock, even for the angel . . .

5. Fire and Ice.

It was a bad dream. It had to be.

My wish didn't come true, I didn't open my eyes and suddenly find myself back in the real world; a world where nobody had died.

Deep down inside, the furnace burned with such ferocity that I could feel myself sliding into the oblivion of vengeance.

I knew what lay ahead of me, because this was the day I would go to war.

The sun rose slowly over the horizon, gradually chasing away the freezing cold of the night as the warmth of daylight took over.

By the time Danny awoke with a shudder, the sun was already high in the sky at around 11 am. The thoughts and his plans for the coming day had played on his mind throughout the night and had taken the form of dreams and nightmares that had become more disturbing with every minute.

At first his surroundings were alien to him and unrecognisable, from the tiny sofa he was crammed onto, to the large television in the corner of the room. He lay there for a couple of minutes as he chased the images away before shrugging the covers off himself and sat up with a groan. His joints ached slightly from the discomfort of the sofa and he snatched up his jeans from the thickly carpeted floor by his left foot.

Several voices issued from a small kitchen to the right, slightly muffled by the thin whitewashed door. Danny threw his jeans on and slowly moved towards the voices. His joints settled down slightly as he took in the familiar orange and white décor of the front room he was in, recognising it as Ade s flat. A strange feeling of comfort came to him and it briefly chased the anger and grief away.

It had been four days since Danny had discharged himself from the hospital. Everybody had banded together to help each other out, something which Danny still remained deeply proud of as he opened the door to the tiny kitchen.

It was a cramped little room with just enough room for two people. In the sink under the window to Danny's right was a small pile of unwashed dishes that Ade had never really got around to doing. He stopped as the two people looked up at him. The first thing Danny noticed was Stacy, her chocolate brown hair falling in a curtain around her shoulder as she turned and gave Danny one of her most dazzling smiles. Her hazel eyes seemed to sparkle as he was taken aback by her beauty once more. It was something he never had been able to get over, something he never could.

Placing her coffee on the marble kitchen side, she strode across to Danny and threw her arms around him.

Ade smiled slightly and inclined his head as Danny wrapped his arms around her waist and kissed her full on the mouth.

"Young love eh?" He teased as they broke apart.

"Don't start," Danny replied quietly. "You really need to get a bigger sofa; my body feels like it's just been stuffed down a drainpipe."

Ade laughed and spun round to put the kettle on and stick some bread in his cut-price white toaster.

"Yeah, give me the money then . . . coffee good for you?"

"Sounds good, Ade thanks."

Danny looked down into Stacy's eyes and smiled before kissing her again. She was his talisman, sending all the feelings of hatred and his thirst for vengeance to the very back of his mind. Even after all this time he loved her like it was their last day. The urge to protect her was stronger than ever, because of what he was about to do.

"Are you planning anything today then Danny?" Ade asked with interest layered in his voice.

Danny looked up but didn't answer immediately.

"Not really, I'll probably just go hiking up to the old hill fort in Winchester," he lied smoothly after a moment.

"Blimey, why would you go there?"

"I just need some peace and quiet mate."

Ade smiled again and spun on his heel, busying himself with the kettle and buttering Danny's toast.

Danny unwound himself from Stacy's embrace and moved across to the kitchen side to grab the plate of toast and coffee from where Ade had just finished. Without realising how hungry he truly was, he wolfed down the toast, the warm bread and butter tasting incredible to him as it went down.

"Ade, I'm going to go and get ready, can you look after Stacy for me?" he murmured as he picked up his cup.

"Of course," Ade replied with a nod.

Danny smiled slightly, his mouth flickering ever so slightly at the sides and left the room with his coffee in hand. It was going to be a long day.

*   *   *

Stewart and Greene left the station just after midday and began to walk the short but heavily beaten track towards the town centre.

They had been hoping to catch Danny on his daily run through the town and were not disappointed when he passed by them as they crossed the old corrugated iron railway bridge that overlooked the station below. Responding to Stewarts hail, Danny slowed to a halt and spun on his heel to face them. Greene immediately noticed the difference from the other times they had passed, in that he wore coal black loose clothes and a set of sturdy hiking boots. He was not out of breath or sweating from the exertion.

"Are you off somewhere, Danny?" Greene asked with a hint of irony to his voice.

Danny's mouth twitched slightly as he held back a smile.

"Yeah, I was going hiking up the old hill fort in Winchester."

Danny was finding the lie easier to tell by the minute, his poker face holding firm as he spoke.

"But why Winchester, there's plenty of places around here you could go hiking, surely?"

Danny felt the force of Greene's stare boring into his eyes. He returned the stare confidently as a slight tingle of suspicion began to arise in the back of his mind. Greene was being too . . . *overbearing*?

Unsure what to make of his questioning, Danny decided to humour him in spite of himself.

"Winchester hill fort means a lot to me-my dad used to take me there when I was a kid."

"And where is your father now?"

For the first time, Danny dropped his gaze and turned away to look out over the old railway station below them. The last time he had seen him had been August 15th 1990, the date of his fourth birthday, when his father, a sergeant in four-two commando the Royal Marines came home to Danny and his mother on three days leave from Bickleigh Barracks. He had run straight into his dad's arms and had then proceeded to take him on his first train journey to the old hill fort his dad had himself loved as a youth.

From the top of the hill, you could see everything for 20 miles in every direction. To the south lay south Hampshire; stretching from Southampton in the west to Portsmouth and Havant in the east. The coastline of the Isle of Wight could be made out on a clear day. Looking to the north, multi-coloured fields sprawled for miles around. It was the only peaceful area Danny had ever known

"Danny?" Stewart asked, becoming concerned as he watched him bow his head in thought. "Are you ok?"

Danny didn't answer right away, still deep in his thoughts.

Eventually he straightened up and faced them as the pain and grief shot across his face.

"Yeah it's just . . ." Danny took a deep calming breath before continuing. "It's just that I haven't seen my dad in sixteen years. He was killed in action during the Gulf War."

"I can imagine it's very hard for you to cope with," Stewart acknowledged in a respectful manner.

"Yeah, look did you want me for something?"

Alex nodded with a slight smile. "I'm afraid so Danny, we need to speak to you about what happened to . . ." his voice trailed off, not wanting to risk forcing Danny away once again.

Alex was very sympathetic towards him, seeing as he wasn't really all that much older than him. Although he couldn't possibly imagine what Danny and his friends were going through, Alex was pretty sure he would have done the same had he been in Danny's shoes.

Danny seemed to hesitate slightly, and Alex suddenly seemed hopeful that Danny would actually comply with his wishes. After a moment he seemed to come to a decision and inclined his head slightly.

"Yeah, I think we should," he replied quietly, "on one condition though . . ."

"And that is?" Alex prompted.

Danny jerked his thumb in Greene's direction, "he goes, and you stay, deal?"

"Now hold on just a minute!" Greene replied angrily, "We are both officers of the law; we decide who interviews you, not you!"

Danny spun to face him. "Right, let me tell you, *DCI Greene;* I don't trust you coppers in the slightest. You want my story, fine, I'll talk. But only to Alex and Alex only."

Greene opened his mouth to reply, but Alex cut him off forcefully.

"David, calm down. If that's what he wishes, then so be it."

Danny grunted his agreement in response. Greene continued to glare furiously at Danny.

"Okay, fine. Just be warned Danny, the next time you mouth off to a police officer I'll have you. Understand me?"

"I'll keep it in mind. Bye then."

Greene continued to grumble as he walked away from them with the air of a man visibly affronted. Danny smirked slightly.

"Sorry about him, he's pretty old school you see," Alex muttered quietly.

"He must be a pain in the arse to work with, clearly."

"Quite, shall we go to the station?" Alex chuckled.

"I'd rather not if you don't mind. I really could do without sitting in that airing cupboard you lot claim to be an interview room. And to be brutally honest, none of you can make a cuppa or a bacon sandwich that tastes anywhere near half decent either!"

"You heard eh?"

"It's common knowledge. Come on; ill educate you on how they're really done."

Alex smiled slightly and followed Danny into town, arriving after several minutes at a shabby looking café situated just off of the high street.

"I think it's fair that I pay, yes?" Danny said quietly as they went inside.

They were immediately hit by the smell of fried food and ketchup and the smell of tea and coffee. Danny rubbed his hands together enthusiastically as he strode forward to the counter where George, a balding man in his fifties waited to take his order.

"Danny!" his voice boomed loudly over the hum. "Not seen you in here for a while mate, where have you been?"

"Had a few things to deal with, how are you mate?" Danny replied, extending his arm to shake hands with a smile.

George dropped his voice slightly as he wringed Danny's hand as though they were old friends. "Yes, well I don't blame you. Sandra was distraught when she heard about Steve."

"She isn't the only one, believe me," Danny murmured. "How are the Grandkids?"

"They're absolutely fine!" George replied in a proud voice as he beamed.

His eighteen year old daughter, Sandra had recently given birth to twins, and George himself had decorated his little café out in all sorts of banners and balloons to commemorate the occasion. Danny remembered it well as he nodded in appreciation before placing his order and gestured to Alex to follow him to the empty booth in the corner.

"I'm guessing you don't get this sort of stuff at the station," Danny said as Alex sat opposite him.

"As if; we've got a prefabricated World War Two style kitchen, a microwave which I brought them last Easter, and a kettle that seems to have been rebuilt from scrap metal," he replied.

Danny grinned. He found it easy to get on with Alex. He was easy going and laid back.

Unlike that arrogant git, Greene, Danny reminded himself quietly.

"Sounds brutal, so what do you want to know?"

Alex settled himself into the old wooden chair as he looked at Danny.

"I need to know everything you know, starting with what actually happened."

Danny didn't smile this time. He had been expecting this, but all the same the memory was so fresh in his mind it was though he could see it playing out in front of his eyes.

"Well, we were just hanging around, as you do. Then out of nowhere this Carter bloke turned up,"

"Up on Middle Park Way, yes?" Alex inquired as he withdrew his notebook from his pocket. He flipped it open as he gestured for Danny to continue.

Danny nodded in reply to Alex's question as George limped over with the sandwiches Danny has paid for. George had been wounded in action during the Falklands War in 1982, hence the limp that had continuously plagued him since.

"Yeah, anyway, he strode up to Jack and asked his name, and when Jack responded Carter pulled a gun on him . . ." Danny paused slightly as the memory hit him like a freight train for what felt like the hundredth time.

"Then Steve threw himself in the way and took the bullets that had been intended for Jack."

"I see," Alex nodded as he jotted down the information. "Forensics examined the scene a few days ago, as you no doubt know.

"They found three blood samples, the first of which was Steve's. The other two we don't yet know about . . ."

"They'll be mine, and Carter's," Danny nodded. "I had to do something before he killed the both of them, so I went for him."

"That would explain the hospital and the cuts and bruises. I'm not sure whether that was very brave or very stupid," Alex replied.

"I'll take that as a compliment," Danny laughed hoarsely.

Alex chuckled. He wished everyone could be as co-operative as Danny finished recounting the story for him.

Silence fell between the two of them as they munched away at their food. After a couple of minutes, Alex spoke again.

"I believe it might have been gang related, even if David doesn't, and we all know the stories about Leigh Park and Eastleigh. I want you to promise me that you won't go over there looking for him, ok? The last thing we need is to have a street war on our hands."

"Agreed," Danny lied, "I give you my word."

Alex nodded and stood up. "Good man. Right, I need to get back, hopefully we can get a match on Carter and we'll find him from there. Thanks for your time."

Danny stood as well, shaking hands with Alex before watching him leave.

When he was gone he fell back into his seat and put his head into his hands.

*   *   *

Darkness fell swiftly as Danny moved through alien streets and attempted to keep a low profile. His eyes combed every inch of his surroundings as he moved from light areas to the darkness in quick calculated movements. His coal black clothes and boots made it easier to blend into the darkness if and when needed.

Eastleigh was a hostile looking place to anybody. It was a town full of run down housing estates that had gone through various regenerations and revamps in a desperate attempt to boost its reputation over the course of its history.

Danny spotted the group ahead of him after several minutes, and with fluid, well-practiced movements he slipped off the pavement and onto the large recreation ground to his right. The darkness swallowed him completely as he avoided the rather large gang of men and boys by a hairs length. Danny followed quickly, silently stalking the group from the safety of the dark darkness. Timing his movement to perfection, he changed his course and picked up his pace to get himself right behind the last of the stragglers. He emerged into the light in the blink of an eye, cupping a hand around the youths mouth to prevent the alarm being raised, he used all the force in his body as his target attempted to resist, pulling him back with strong, sure hands, yanking his arm to the point of pain as it twisted behind his back.

"Hello there," Danny whispered as the darkness engulfed them both. The youth struggled furiously against his hold. Danny adjusted his grip slightly, nudging the lads arm up ever so slightly that he whimpered and groaned with the pain.

"Stop resisting me and it'll be less painful," Danny growled with a threatening edge to his voice.

The lad slowly stopped his struggling.

"Good boy, now I want some information from you. Think you can manage that?"

The hatred Danny had for this lad, the apathy he felt towards his enemy stood as the dominant emotions in his mind. The lad stood stock still, so he continued.

"Four days ago, one of your mates attacked me and my friends in Leigh Park, killing one of them. I want to know where Carter is, right now!"

The lad began struggling as soon as he heard the name. It was the one name that would ever make the young lad so suddenly fearful and desperate to flee. Danny notched up the pressure on the arm just an extra bit more, drawing an agonised scream of pain from the teenager in front of him before he finally settled down. Danny removed his hand from the lad's mouth so he could speak and the words began tumbling out of the youngster's mouth as the fear took over completely.

"I didn't know, I swear! Whoever it was can't be one of us, we would never dream . . ."

"Well someone did!" Danny interrupted furiously. "Some scumbag Eastleigh boy attacked us and I want to know where he is!"

"I don't know who . . . I swear," cried the lad.

Danny twitched the arm again and the teenager screamed once more.

"This is your last chance, tell me where Carter is, or I'll break your arm," he growled as the anger picked up inside him, hitting a crescendo and blinding him with rage.

"I don't fucking know who that guy-"

An almighty snap issued from the young lad's upper arm as Danny tweaked it with real force, snapping the bone as he had promised. He let out a real animal scream of pain as the bone protruded through the skin as Danny let go of the teenager and let him fall to the floor as he howled in agony.

Danny looked down at him with the air of absolute disgust. He can't have been more than eighteen, but Danny didn't care. He felt no emotion over the pain he had caused as he turned away.

*   *   *

Carter stood in the main control area overlooking the huge map once more. The radio chatter between his cell and the other cells across the country echoed around the dilapidated old barn. As he had done for the past three days, he stared non-stop at one area alone.

His thoughts slipped back to the only day he had ever felt remorseful for his actions, back to a time when he had been young and reckless. The actions that had now brought the son of Colin Patterson into his life ensured that if he ever found out about the events of sixteen years ago, it would kill him.

The mobile rang just after 8pm, disturbing Carter from his train of thought. Recognising the number with a slight smile, he answered the call.

"Yes?"

It's started, your little stunt in Leigh Park worked.

The caller's voice was gruff and full of experience as he spoke.

"Have you any details?" Carter asked.

All my contact told me was that one of the lads whose mate you killed went hunting for you. A group of twenty got to the end of the main road in and out of Eastleigh to find they were a man down.

Carter raised his eyebrows in surprise. "Do you know who it was?"

No one knows, but I believe it may have been a man called Danny Patterson. I did some digging after I spoke with him earlier, and it turns out that his old man was an old comrade of yours. There was a chase across the town when others spotted him, but he got away.

Although a CCTV camera did catch an image of him, albeit a grainy one. Whoever he is, he is after you.

"Send me the image," Carter growled he strode across the floor to the nearest Laptop. He already had his suspicions, and on this one and only occasion, he fervently hoped he was wrong.

It's done.

The CCTV image was, as promised, extremely grainy and unclear as it popped up on the screen.

"Clean that up," he ordered the young technician who was in front of the laptop. Obediently he ran the program to clear up the pixels and zoomed into the figure's face.

Carter's suspicions were immediately confirmed as he stared into the face of Danny Patterson. The red mist of anger descended instantly as he finally recognised how much of a potential threat Danny could be to The Rogues. He had to be stopped.

"That's him. Take him out. *Now!*" he ordered before hanging up.

Carter steeled himself for the coming storm. Grabbing his long trench coat and checking his weapon, he hurried out of the barn and made for his car.

*   *   *

Danny finally settled down as the train pulled into Bedhampton tiny little station, hovering by the door until the last moment and alighting to the platform just as the pneumatic doors began to close. He remained alert even though he was alone, his eyes constantly scanning the scene and moving swiftly out of the station and on to the deserted street. In the back of his mind, the survival skills he had learned since the day he was able to walk kicked into overdrive. He kept moving, constantly keeping alert to any and every movement as he strode down empty streets and back towards the safety of home. His mobile beeped once to indicate a text message. The number was one he didn't recognise.

Taking an extra cautious glance behind him, he opened the message:

> *Danny, I need to talk to you as a matter of urgency. I believe I may have discovered where your friend's killer is and I need your help to bring him down.*
>
> *Come to my house on Bedhampton Road, no. 224. I'll meet you there. Alex Stewart.*

He frowned as he read the message over again and again. Questions began popping into his mind. Was this a trap? Was this the truth, and Stewart *had* found Carter after all?

No matter how Danny looked at it, he couldn't answer those questions as he hesitated.

6. The Betrayal

Something didn't feel right, as though I was being followed, tested. I couldn't help but worry that something was about to happen. I had to be on my guard.

The world was changing. I could see it in a new way and I could tell that it would never be the same again.

It was dead quiet as Danny made his way through the streets. After twenty minutes, he reached his destination, slowing his pace as the suspicion flickered in his mind once more. He began to edge slowly closer as every sense warned Danny to run, to turn away and flee.

The house lay before him, half hidden in the night. A semi-detached place, it lay about half way up the two mile road.

Danny remained alert as he moved up the drive way and past the little Citroen Saxo parked up there. There was no light issuing from the windows, and Danny's nose flared as an incredibly strong and sickly smell hit him. He halted as he inhaled it, brow furrowing with confusion as he recognised the pungent smell of Petroleum.

Danny was sure to judge his next move carefully. Alarm bells began to ring in the back of his mind, and that unnatural urge to flee kicked in for the second time as he thoroughly scanned the scene. After making sure the street was empty, he moved towards the door.

Almost immediately he noticed the front door was ajar and stretched out his hand, pushing the door open and stepped inside. The door swung shut behind him, engulfing him in the darkness as he was hit by the pungent smell of the petrol once again, twice as strong as before. The silence was the only thing that greeted him, a silence that made him incredibly uneasy.

"Alex?" Danny called out. "It's Danny; I got your text . . ."

There was no reply, and so Danny began to move through the house, slowly checking the kitchen and then heading into to the moderate sized front room. He glanced fleetingly at the pictures of Alex and a faired haired woman who he recognised as one of the forecourt assistants from the garage just up the road. He spotted the ring on her finger and realised almost immediately that she was Alex's wife.

Confusion reigned in Danny's mind; the house seemed to be deserted. Why would Stewart send him a text when he wasn't even in? It was the floorboard creaking overhead that alerted Danny to a presence within the house. He moved silently towards the staircase, placing his right foot on the bottom step as he hesitated.

"Hello?" Danny called again.

Using the soft carpet to his advantage, he made his way upstairs, emerging onto the landing where the petrol smell was at its strongest. Carefully, he made his way into the master bedroom, and froze.

Alex Stewart was sprawled across the floor, next to the slight figure of the woman from the photo; their eyes were wide open and accusing. Danny sprinted across the room, vaulting over the tiny bedside table to get to them.

Stewart had a single gunshot wound to the side of his head. His mousy brown hair was matted and wet with the blood that slowly drained from the wound.

"No, no, no!" Danny groaned as he crouched down in a vain attempt to find Stewarts pulse.

This can't be happening.

Stewart was dead, Danny could tell that immediately. The wound he had received had been fatal. Danny repeated the routine on Stewart's wife, with no success. He rocked backwards, collapsing against the unmade double bed and holding his head in his hands.

He felt defeated and alone. Whoever Carter was, he was cruel, and as cold as ice. First Steve, and now this . . .

If it was the last thing he did, Danny swore to himself that he would bring Carter down, no matter the cost. He stood up slowly, looking down at Stewart's body, and looking into his empty eyes. What had been Stewart's crime?

Another noise; louder and more pronounced, followed by the unmistakable metallic click of a weapons safety catch being flicked off. Danny spun on his heel to face the newcomer, standing still as he stared into the assassin's eyes. Even in the darkness, he recognised them instantly.

"Why?" Danny growled.

"Why?" echoed David Greene from the darkness. "You really don't know?"

"That's why I'm asking," Danny snapped.

He eyed the gun in Greene's hand; A Beretta 92, the dark silver finish was just visible in the darkness. A silencer was attached to the barrel and was aimed at Danny's torso. With an effective range of 50 metres, a single round could pass straight through Danny's body like a blowtorch through butter and still have enough power to embed itself in the wall behind him.

"Alex here grew a little suspicious about what's really happening, so I had to take him out. It was a shame really, because I liked him."

"So what? You were protecting him from the truth?"

Greene chuckled.

"You could say that, Danny. If the *truth* came out now, if the country found out what was coming . . ."

"I suppose Carter's in on this, is he?" Danny asked.

In his heart, he knew this was Carter's work. Without thinking, without fear or concern for his well-being, he began to move slowly towards Greene.

"Carter wants you dead for some reason. He sees you as a real threat to our cause," Greene replied. He began to fidget slightly as Danny edged closer, gripping the gun in his hand tighter than before.

"Well in that case, I'll make sure I kill him before he kills me then," he growled.

Greene pulled out a silver lighter from his pocket, lighting it and holding it aloft.

Danny stopped. He was in easy reaching distance of Greene now. He judged his options as he played for time.

"I trusted you and Alex, because you asked me to. Havant trusted you; Hampshire and the rest of this country trusted you, as an officer of the law to protect the people. You're a joke, Greene. A disappointment," he said quietly, putting as much venom and hatred into his voice as he could muster.

"I'd advise you to step back Danny, before I send us both to hell."

Danny remained where he was. Greene held his ground without fear.

"Do it Greene, I dare you."

"This is your last warning Patterson!"

"DO IT!" Danny roared as the anger finally broke through, "Do it and prove that you aren't a coward!"

Greene smiled as his courage built up, before letting the flame fall. It hit the ground, igniting the petrol with gusto. It raced forward, taking hold in less than a second. The flames threw both Danny and Greene into sharp relief, and for just a second they stared furiously at each other. Greene squeezed the trigger, and Danny made his move, grabbing the weapon and forcing it upwards as the first bullet exploded from the chamber and slammed into the ceiling. Greene readjusted his balance and fought back against Danny's superior strength. They struggled, impulsively, Greene depressed the trigger again, firing a second bullet into the ceiling and showering both of them with masonry.

The fire began to take hold at the opposite side of the room, ominously snaking closer to Danny and Greene as they fought. Danny forced Greene off balance again, shoving him into the wall and knocking the weapon out of his hands. It fell to the floor at Danny's feet, and he kicked it away, sending it spinning out of the room. It clattered noisily down the stairs, hitting the bottom step and firing itself as Greene struggled up and came at Danny with a ferocity that defied his age.

Dodging Greene's right hook, he counter attacked, lunging forwards and catching Greene in the side of the ribs, striking him several times with all the force he could muster. Grabbing him at the back of his collar, he threw him across the burning bedside table and backed away as the flames grew closer. Greene quickly shook off the blows, scrambling up and leaping over the flames, charging into Danny from the right hand side and sending them sprawling into the hall. The flames were right behind them, as though they were eager to join in the fight.

They struggled up and Greene landed a fierce kick into Danny's gut, throwing him onto his back. Greene held him against the ground, pinning him and throwing punch after punch. Danny absorbed the blows, feeling the warm wet flow of blood beginning to well up from the wound on his right cheek and shifted his weight, throwing Greene off him and springing agilely to his feet.

They came to blows again as the flames engulfed the place where they had been moments before. Danny threw himself off balance dodging the first attack, but stumbled as the follow up connected with his face. Greene, sensing the advantage grabbed Danny as he attempted to recover, dragging him to the edge of the staircase as the fire closed in. A portion of the floor gave in, collapsing down to the bottom of the house where the fire began to swiftly take hold. Greene's hands closed in on Danny's neck as they grappled.

"Do it, Greene. Finish the job!" Danny taunted over the roar of the flames. Greene laughed

"Steve is waiting for you Danny, I'm sure he must be looking forwards to seeing his cowardly friend."

"Not today," Danny growled. He brought his leg up into Greene's stomach, forcing him to lose his grip and double back. He recovered quickly and aimed a kick that sent Danny sprawling down the stairs.

He groaned with agony as he hit the floor, struggling to recover from the fall as Greene began scrambling down the stairs to finish the job.

Danny caught the glint of the flames off the gun that had come to rest at the bottom of the stairs and out of desperation he scrambled across the floor to snatch the weapon up. Spinning around and raising the weapon, he pulled the trigger.

The gun kicked back angrily as the bullet shot out of the chamber, and Danny looked on in horror as it hit Greene in the neck, ripping straight through the tissue and muscle and exiting the opposite side. The blood began to drain from his face as Greene froze, his eyes blank as the life left his body.

It seemed to take an age for his body to fall, collapsing and hitting the floor at his feet. Danny stood there, gun extended as he attempted to comprehend what he had just done. The flames roared closer, closing in on the gas pipes. Seconds later a strange pop issued from the kitchen, bringing Danny back down to earth as the smell of gas hit him. Spinning on his heel and ripping open the front door he threw himself out of the building as it exploded. The blast ripped the house apart, taking the houses on both sides of it as well. The sheer force of the explosion flattened Danny against the concrete as the car was thrown into the middle of the road, rolling onto its roof and exploding into flames.

Danny struggled slowly to his feet as bits of flaming debris rained down on him. His body felt battered and abused as he stumbled forward, gasping for air as the pain raged through his body and clutching subconsciously at the unfamiliar weapon in his left hand. He turned around after a few seconds and was horrified by what he saw.

The explosion had all but destroyed Stewarts house. The flames roared at least thirty feet into the air, throwing off a tremendous amount of heat that flashed towards him in swift unforgiving waves.

Danny slowly turned away and froze as Carter strode towards him. They made for their weapons, aiming at each other with equal looks of hatred.

"You just won't take the hint, will you?" Carter growled as he came to a halt at the end of the driveway.

Danny laughed. "What's the excuse this time?"

"Stewart threatened my organisation . . . as do you," Carter replied with a slight sneer. The threat in his voice was unmistakeable.

"And what about his wife, or didn't you know that he *had* a life?"

"She was witness and a potential liability."

"SHE WAS INNOCENT!" Danny snarled.

"Yet you blew them to hell, Yes Danny, YOU!" Carter retorted as he glanced accusingly at the remnants of the houses behind Danny. "The police are on their way to arrest you for their murders. Greene made sure of that."

"I'm sure he did," Danny spat furiously.

"You shouldn't have got yourself involved Danny. Now, I'm going to offer you a choice . . . flee now, leave and never return or interfere in the affairs of The Rogues again, or we will continue to strike against you, beginning with that beautiful young woman you have on your arm."

"How's about I kill you? Right here, right now," Danny responded furiously.

Carter smiled slightly.

"You could, but my people *will* retaliate by taking out Miss Ryan. Please bear in mind that the police will be here in about a minute," Carter replied loftily, with an almost business-like edge to his voice.

Danny grappled with the thoughts in his head, the emotions that plagued him and haunting him like his own personal poltergeist. He kept seeing the bullet connecting with Greene's neck, replaying in slow motion as it tortured him again and again. Was he justified in his killing? Was it his right?

Danny knew he couldn't answer. He began to lower the weapon as he continued to glare wildly at Carter.

"I want your word, *your word* that she will not be harmed," Danny growled quietly.

"Give me your word in return, then yes. You have my word."

Danny fought the urge to admit defeat without success. Slowly, hesitantly, he lowered his weapon.

The first police car shot up the street towards them, its sirens blocking out the roaring sound of the fire that raged behind Danny and Carter. It was joined swiftly by several more identical vehicles, pulling up on the side of the road, creating a metal cul-de-sac around them.

Defeat was not an option, it never had been. He looked Carter fully in the eyes as the police surrounded them and the urge to live began to take over as the dominant thought in Danny's mind.

"I don't know what you want, Carter, and to be honest I don't really care, but you crossed a line. I *will* be back for you", he snarled as he raised the weapon for the second time.

"The game begins then," Carter replied.

Danny diverted his aim to the right and opened fire. The weapon kicked back with the discharge, expelling the round into the fuel tank of Carter's 4x4. The petrol ignited as the gunpowder exploded, sending the fireball ripping through the vehicle like a blowtorch through butter. The shockwave was powerful enough to send Carter sprawling to the ground, along with the police officers closest to them.

Spotting an opening, Danny spun on his heel and ran, sprinting flat out into the dark alleyway that lay to his left.

Danny refused to stop running; it felt like the smoke and the harsh smell of burning wood and petroleum was chasing him, desperate to drag him back to the scene to make him face what he had done.

Stewart had done nothing wrong, and he wasn't a threat to anyone. Why Carter would kill him was well beyond Danny.

He picked up the pace as the sound of more sirens joined the chase, and his throat began to burn from the lack of oxygen. He didn't slow down.

*   *   *

Carter strolled briskly away from the burning houses, brushing off the ash and dust from his suit as he did so.

He had to admit, that had been a smart move of Danny's and there was no way he could have anticipated it.

The first rule of combat: know your enemy. That very saying had been drilled into him from the day he had begun basic training with the Parachute Regiment. After two meetings with Danny it had become clear that he would be a fervent thorn in his side, but at the same time Carter was intrigued by him.

Danny seemed to have a commanding presence about him, albeit reckless and inexperienced. He stuck to the old reputation that the local area had; in that he was incredibly loyal and didn't seem to know the meaning of the word 'defeat.' Danny was no doubt Colin's son and that unnerved Carter slightly.

It had been his fault that Colin Patterson had never made it home from the Gulf. His team had been sent in to take out Saddam Hussein and Carter himself had been 'loaned' by the Firm and placed into the unit due to his shooting ability and navigational skills. The squad had even nicknamed themselves 'The Rogues'. It was ironic; they had been put together by the deniable operations section for a mission that was after all, strictly off the record. They were splinter cells who ran off the grid, just like The Increment . . .

No, in fact they *were* part of The Increment.

At just twenty two, Carter had been the youngest employee of the SIS in its history. Of course he knew the story: SIS headhunted young squaddies for operations that they weren't expected to return from in one piece. He knew the type; the orphans did the dying whilst the Eton boys with stiff upper lips and expensive watches sat in positions of power signing the death warrants time and time again. There had been a time during the Cold War when it was the old war heroes and posh lads who went out to spy on their communist enemies. The good old days of James Bond and George Smiley and the world was just that little bit saner that it was today.

The fallout from the disaster had been catastrophic, and the country had been humiliated. Of course as the only survivor, Carter became the scapegoat and the chew toy of a pissed off government and a humiliated SIS. There had been no denying the operation, with one of the captured operatives confessing live on television to a shocked world before being shot in the head and beheaded. Of course they had *tried* to deny it at the time, even attempted to pass it off as an American hit squad . . . god knows they love a good war.

As soon as the fallout had passed, the army had drummed him out of the corps and he had been cast out into the wilderness; A gun for hire in a hostile world. He had sworn revenge on those smug, arrogant toe rags. The fuck up hadn't been his fault, but had in turn been pretty unavoidable with crappy intelligence from the spooks at Thames House.

Carter shook the memory out of his mind, choosing instead to concentrate on the matter at hand. Danny was on the run, fleeing from his destiny, *the coward.*

Carter thought about simply going to the source of the problem and face him head on, but decided against it. Why provoke another battle when he could use the full might of The Rogues against him instead?

Corner him and leave him defenceless. That was the answer. It was a case of survival of the fittest and this "game" would not end until one of them stood victorious over the others body. Carter ducked swiftly into a dark alley, pulling his mobile from his inner breast pocket and thumbing the speed dial button. Keeping it brief, he put the word out on Danny, issuing the capture-or-kill order to his unit, who would then send the same order to every cell. Ending the call with a request for extraction, he snapped the phone shut and pocketed it.

* * *

Stacy was worried again. Danny had been due home well over an hour ago yet he still hadn't returned. She got up from the sofa for the umpteenth time and paced around restlessly, ranging from the windows of the second floor flat they lived in to the front door. The same feeling kept surfacing in her mind and chilling her blood to limit as with the thought that maybe, *just maybe*, Danny had met that Carter again. The thought scared her, absolutely terrified her. He had come away from his first meeting with that killer incredibly fortunately; he had almost killed Danny. This time he may not be so lucky.

She was shaken from her thoughts by the explosion, the noise waking up the entire neighbourhood. She rushed to the window, ripping open the curtains and gasping in horror as she saw the flames and smoke rising from a group of houses just ten minutes' walk away. Was Danny involved? Was Carter?

She turned away as she fought to keep herself in control. She dropped onto the sofa after a while and put her head in her hands as she continued to worry.

When the door banged open a few minutes later, she jumped in fright as it snapped her out of her thoughts. She saw Danny standing in front of her, out of breath and covered in . . .

Soot! The voice in Stacy's head cried as she stared at him. *So the fire had involved him and Carter after all.*

"Danny?" she asked quietly and slightly timidly as she took in his appearance.

Had he been running?

He was covered in sweat, and inhaling deeply as though trying to catch his breath, blood welled from a large cut on the side of his face. "What happened?"

"Carter laid a trap, killed Stewart and his wife in order to could get to me."

Danny strode into the kitchen there and then, Stacy followed him.

He began to shake as he slapped a towel to his face and began cleaning up the blood.

"It was all Greene. He worked for Carter . . . tried to kill me too. I'm a threat to him Stace, A real threat," Danny stammered quickly. "He's a threat to me too, and to you. I've got to leave, run now while I've still got the chance."

Stacy gaped at him. She had never once seen him this way. He seemed scared; absolutely and truthfully scared. He had always been cool under pressure, always winning out in the end. For the first time she noticed the gun on the side, glistening ever so slightly against the light.

"Danny, please. Tell me what happened. Why have you got a gun?" She asked a little too forcefully.

Danny froze.

"Greene turned on me. I had to defend myself Stace, you must understand that!" he replied as he spun to face her.

It was then that she saw the fear etched in his face, and she knew; *Greene was dead, and Danny was the killer.*

"I tried to get out, I tried to run," he continued, "but he was right on top of me. I snatched that up. And I *shot* him."

His face contorted in pain as the memory flashed before his eyes.

"Get Bill, I need to speak to him. And tell him what's happened," he told her quietly after a moment.

Stacy did as she was asked, disappearing out of the kitchen and leaving him alone.

He rushed around, changing his clothes and shoving the old ones in a bin bag. He'd dispose of them when the time was right.

I'm not a killer, he told himself over and over again.

The minutes passed slowly as he waited. Hopefully she would be on her way back up with Bill by now . . .

He picked up the weapon from the side and stared at it, hoping somewhat vainly that he would suddenly lose the memory of his first kill.

Perhaps Ade *was* right; Danny wasn't a natural killer, he couldn't bear it.

Bill shot through into the kitchen there and then, looking at the weapon in his hands with an expression of horror.

"Danny?" he asked quickly as Stacy joined him.

"It's happened Bill. I need your car and as much cash as possible," Danny replied quickly. He was sure he didn't have much time left before the police swooped down on them.

"Are you sure about this? Stacy needs you here. She needs your protection."

"No, I'm the target now, I'm better off away from here . . . it's the only way."

Stacy looked at Danny in horror, unable to believe that he would actually flee and leave her alone.

"I'm coming with you," She told him firmly.

Danny shook his head

"No, I can't guarantee your safety. As soon as I leave, they'll be right on top of me. You're safer *here* where Bill can protect you," he replied just as firmly.

"I'll be out of touch for a while. I'll send word to you when I can."

Bill watched him, and after a few seconds handed over what Danny had requested of him.

Danny quickly kissed Stacy full on the mouth. It was a kiss that lingered, but at the same time was desperate; *fearful*.

Danny said his goodbyes quickly and then strode quickly out of the flat.

He was extra careful on the way out of the building. It seemed like Carter was dogging his every move, hiding in every shadow waiting for his chance to snuff out Danny's life just as he had Steve's. There had been no remorse, no mercy and no inclination at all that he was an innocent party who had friends and a family.

Carter had already won. Danny wanted to give up, quit and let him get away with murder. He could return to the quiet life that he'd dreamed of. He could watch Stacy sleeping peacefully and not have to worry about the vicious new world that had so suddenly surrounded him. *Was it really too much to ask?*

Danny snapped out of his thoughts and ran, sprinting to the car park in front of him and locating Bills new car in a heartbeat. He thumbed the button on the key, and the little Nissan Almera flashed its indicators in response as it unlocked its doors for him. He shoved the binbag of clothes in the back and clambered into the driver's seat. Despite not owning a drivers licence himself, he had driven this car several times in the past on off-roading tracks and private property.

The engine purred as it started up. It felt eager to begin moving, a ton of power and speed all locked in a two litre engine. The Almera itself was quite fast for the diesel model that it was.

Under the bonnet lay a two litre CD20 "straight 4" turbo charged Diesel engine that packed a lot of punch and a lot of speed. The turbo itself kicked in at speed, boosting its performance nicely. Almeras were extremely capable of keeping up with BMW's and lower range Subaru's despite its classification as a family car.

Danny threw the gear into reverse, backing up quickly before moving up to first and heading out of the car park. He hit the main road out of the area within minutes, flooring it and making for the motorway without a backwards glance.

* * *

"Where is he going?" asked Stacy for the hundredth time.
"Stace, I don't know!" Bill replied angrily.

In the half hour period that had passed, Stacy had broken down, calmed down and then smashed a mirror in frustration. Of course Bill couldn't blame her.

The events of the last few days had really taken their toll on her, more than the rest of them. She was tough, incredibly so, able to shoulder whatever her life had thrown at her. Together she and Danny had been through a lot, and it had been a sign of their strength and their loyalty and love for each other that they had survived until now.

But this was different. Danny was locked in a struggle with Steve's murderer. Both of them had a vendetta against each other, and whilst Danny's was personal, Carter's motives remained unknown. Bill had never seen her so scared . . . Danny was the only one who was able to calm her down, which had been proven in the several years they had been together.

"I don't like this Bill, it feels wrong," she murmured quietly.

"You and me both, Danny needs us to remain strong though, Stace. He's doing this to protect you!"

"I should be with him."

"As long as Carter's alive *you* are the target, just as much as Danny is," he told her.

Stacy shuddered and gave a tiny squeak of fear before she jumped up from the sofa once again, pacing around for what Bill reckoned was the ninth time.

"He needs me with him, he needs me there in that car with him he won't come back I need him to come back . . ."

Bill jumped up as she broke down in tears again, taking her in his arms carefully and attempting to console her.

"Stacy, listen to me . . . listen! Danny will come back for you, he IS coming back. He'll take Carter down and then you two will be free. We'll all be able to move on with our lives."

"I'd be safer with him . . ." she continued to babble on.

"No you won't. Carter is going to hit him with *everything* he's got and he won't be able to protect you when he's concentrating on preserving his own life," Bill cut her off forcefully.

He believed in Danny, believed in his ability to stay alive. Carter would be killed and then everyone involved would be able to go about their business once more. Life would return back to normal and they would be able to finally put Steve's memory to rest.

Without a doubt, they were in for the long haul. Bill just hoped that Danny *would* survive.

*   *   *

The hours passed by slowly, as though time was on Danny's side, fighting against them. Carter remained at the communications desk with Harcourt non-stop. They were waiting for news of any sighting, and any possible lead that might lead them to Danny. The entire cell remained alert. Just in case. Even though Carter knew Danny wouldn't attempt a head on assault; he couldn't help but put it past him. He knew he was reckless in his youth, but from what he had seen he knew his stuff and was without a doubt his father's son.

The atmosphere was tense and incredibly so, but even then nobody relaxed, or even attempted to slack off. They had too much at stake.

*   *   *

Danny reached the border at 5am. The sun hadn't risen yet and it seemed incredibly dark. After six hours hard driving, he needed a rest, and he needed fuel. He set about locating an open petrol station, keeping the speed down as he entered Scotland.

*   *   *

Carter was used to battling the temptation to sleep, and as the years had passed he'd found it continually easier to fight it. He felt sluggish as dawn approached, even if it wasn't anything he couldn't handle. Outside he could see the sun beginning to make its climb up from the horizon to the east and at 6:30am the radio hissed and fuzzed slightly before the message he had waited for the entire night arrived:

> *Patterson spotted on Scottish border two miles north of Gretna, Permission to engage?*

Carter savoured the moment. After an entire night of waiting it was finally time to end it, to destroy the last of the worry from his mind with the death of Danny Patterson.

"Granted, Proof of the kill please," he replied.

He wouldn't be taking any chances. Danny was a slippery character there was no doubt about that. Breathing a huge sigh of relief, Carter made his way back towards the tea area for a strong cup of coffee.

7. Edinburgh

What had I done? Life had just shown me its trump card. It had shown me just how lethal, harsh and unfair the world was.

I wasn't a killer; I didn't have a heart as cold as ice. I kept seeing the bullet wipe the life from Greene's eyes. Kept seeing that fearful, accusing stare etched onto Alex and his wife's faces.

The remorse tore at me. It was slowly killing me and it felt like it was about to consume and destroy me for ever.

The sun was rising as Danny travelled through Edinburgh city centre. He kept strictly to the speed limits as he passed through already busy streets, with commuters making their way to and from work.

It was coming up for 7:30am and the urge to sleep tore at Danny incessantly. He hadn't slept for well over twenty four hours and as a result he was pretty drowsy, fighting tooth and nail to remain alert as he looked for a place to stop and grab a little bit of shut eye.

His thoughts began to drop back to Stacy, wondering idly if she was okay.

Of course she is you daft git, the little voice in his head told him.

Danny trusted Bill with his life, even more so now that he was on the run. Bill would protect her with everything he had. Such was the affection that everyone shared towards Stacy; she was too loveable, perhaps for her own good. After three years together, Danny still couldn't believe how very lucky he was to have a girl like Stacy on his arm. He and Bill had fought for her then, and they both fought for her now.

His thoughts now drove round to Carter. What exactly was the deal with him?

Danny just couldn't fathom out what connected the two of them, like Fire and Ice. There was something more, an ulterior motive that had brought them together. That worried him slightly, as Carter didn't seem like a petty gangster with an axe to grind. Danny couldn't help but think that whatever it was, it involved *him* somehow.

Danny suddenly snapped out of it, slamming on the brakes and just about avoiding being sideswiped by the first bus of the day. Feeling unnerved as the bus driver shouted a stream of curses at him he pulled off the road and into a petrol station. He parked up quickly and clambered out of the car, not noticing the trio of black Alfa Romeo Breras pull in as well. Danny put his head in his hands, exhaling deeply as he attempted to calm himself down. He was surprised that he had made it this far without incident, maybe Carter wasn't as all powerful as he'd made himself out to be after all. He'd expected to be hit from all sides by an invisible army or something almost as soon as he had made a run for it. He grew frustrated, slamming his hands down against the steering wheel angrily as he thought about it. Then again, was Carter a man of his word? Would he keep his promise to leave Stacy alone, if he stayed away?

He couldn't answer that question. Feeling apprehensive, he clambered out of his car and entered the shop, grabbing a couple of cans of Red Bull from the chiller in an effort to wake himself up and paid for them at the till where the grumpy old attendant grumbled away to nobody in particular.

Danny downed the first can before he left the shop, shoving the empty can in the bin on the forecourt and opening the second. He stopped to admire the sleek looking cars on the other side but even then he felt uneasy, like he was being watched and his every move followed.

He shuddered slightly, scanning the environment for danger before striding quickly back to his car. He threw himself into the driver's seat, glancing back at the Alfa's and then it clicked: *three of them, parallel to each other, the same make, and the same model.*

Danny recognised the danger there and then, starting the engine, and accelerated quickly out of the petrol station; the Red Bull lay forgotten, discarded in the foot well of the passenger seat.

Danny glanced into the rear view mirror and saw the Alfa's closing in as they chased him through the streets. He blew through a red light, racing the Alfas through the junction and smiling as the third car was ploughed by a Defender jeep as the traffic moved across their path.

Danny struggled to believe it had taken them this long to find him, realising then with a pang of disbelief that they had been following him since he had passed through Gretna.

How the hell didn't I spot them earlier?

The Alfa Romeo's had the edge in terms of speed, always catching up to the little Nissan Almera before Danny swerved in an attempt to shake them off. The two surviving Alfas began to open fire, and the chatter of the machine guns was lost in the roar of the engines as the three cars duelled. Rounds pinged off the bodywork of the Almera, forcing Danny to duck as the back windows were smashed and shattered by the bullets. Danny responded, playing fate as he returned fire blindly at the chasing Breras, he didn't dare look back as the Almera hit a 100mph. The slide locked back as the last bullet went flying off in the direction of the two Breras, and Danny threw the gun into the passenger foot well before pushing the car to even quicker speeds. The car continually bucked and careened as it swerved in and out of the traffic, with Danny only just keeping control as the Forth Bridge bore down on him. He came under fire once more as the chasers raced him onto the bridge itself.

The Firth of Forth was a tidal estuary, connecting the Forth River to the North Sea. Geologically, the Firth was a Fjord, created by the Forth Glacier during the last Ice Age and acted as a natural border, separating the City of Edinburgh, West Lothian and East Lothian in the South, from Fife in the North. The Road Bridge that spanned it was a suspension bridge that connected Edinburgh at South Queensferry to North Queensferry in Fife.

Opened in 1964, it replaced an ancient ferry service that originally connected the area around the Forth.

Danny pushed the car to its top speed, flying across the bridge with both Breras hot on his tail. More bullets rained down on him as he began to grow desperate. Spotting an opening, he threw the car onto the opposite side of the road, now dodging incoming traffic at speeds well in excess of 125mph. The second of the Breras slammed into the same truck that Danny had narrowly missed a millisecond earlier, getting smashed into pieces as the truck hit it head on. With one Brera left, Danny began to feel more confident as they tore back onto the left hand side of the road.

The duel had been punishing, deadly. But Danny had to end it somehow; there was no getting away from a car like the Alfa Romeo Brera and he knew it as they rocketed off the bridge and into Dunfermline. Danny slowed slightly, forcing the Brera to slow with him as he blocked him in. he sped up once more, and allowed the Brera to come alongside. He saw the driver glance at him and the passenger next to him raised his gun as he prepared to fire. Danny swerved, smashing the cars together and knocking the shooter's aim awry. They clashed again, attempting to force each other off the road as another major intersection approached, *closer, and closer.*

They rifled through the red light and met the traffic crossing their path. The Brera was the first to go as several cars smashed into its passenger side and spinning it furiously into the middle of the road, clipping the Almera as it went. The Almera's wheels lost its grip on the road surface as it slid and the body lifted from the road, flipping several times and eventually coming to rest on its roof near the central reservation.

The traffic slowed to a halt in the midst of the devastation and there was nothing but silence.

*   *   *

Carter followed the events of the morning obsessively, his focus wholly devoted to hearing the news he so desperately wanted. He wanted to be there, wanted be leading the charge so that he could take down Danny himself. He had never been so obsessed about any other kill, any threat that he had faced in the past.

It didn't come as a surprise when his allies in Scotland reported him cornered in a petrol station in Edinburgh. They knew what they were doing, and as the kids said; *it was their turf.*

Carter expected confirmation of the kill within minutes, feeling as though it had been a weight pressing him down into the earth, or a pair of hands strangling him. That pressure was about to be lifted, and he would be free again.

Of course aside from that, he had other issues on his plate. The Rogues were pushing forward with their operation, and they expected a successful conclusion within the week. They had been working towards it for years, never truly attempting a large scale attack of this nature before now. The Rogues themselves were all made up of current armed forces personnel and ex personnel. For ten years they had remained hidden in the shadows, planning and plotting.

Carter had joined up when they first started, beginning as rumours within the military and intelligence communities. As soon as he had heard them, he went looking and was inducted into the secretive community on the spot. The Rogues had been responsible for a lot of the countries recent events over the last ten years, adept at creating political and civilian unrest in order to achieve their aims.

It therefore came as a huge surprise to both Carter and Harcourt when the message filtered through that Danny was-in fact, not cornered at all. He had got back to his car, spotted the tail and then made a run for it. As the chase played out over the comms link, Carter couldn't help but admire Danny for his persistence and his courage. He felt almost ashamed to be doing this. Danny had a real martial zeal about him and he would have done well in the Organisation. Maybe he would have even met Fairfax.

Carter showed no emotion as the crackling sound of gunfire issued throughout the room, mixing in with the fierce snarling sound of high performance engines being put through their paces.

Next to him, Harcourt was a little taken aback but quickly recovered as the news came in that one of their cars were down and that Danny was running for the Forth road bridge.

More gunfire issued around the room, piercing the thoughts of every man in it. The chase roared onto the road bridge as the chasers reported the fact that they were now under fire. For a few seconds the comms fell silent, antagonizing the atmosphere even further. The sound of the crash echoed around the room and then more silence. Then after a few seconds;

> Patterson swerved, got round the side of a HGV that just wiped car two out, no Survivors! I repeat-no survivors!

Carter cursed, pummelling the desk in front of him in anger. There was no doubt in his mind now. Danny Patterson was truthfully his father's son. He was good, impossibly good for a young man like him. One car remained in the chase as they entered Fife. The comms crackled again.

> Entering Dunfermline, Patterson is slowing and blocking us . . .

Carter grabbed the mike furiously,
"Either get alongside, or shoot the tires!"

> Alongside, aiming . . .

The next thing they heard was the harsh banging sound of metal on metal, and it continued for half a minute. A second later, a huge smashing sound, accompanied by the screams of the men filled the room. They were bloodcurdling, drawn out screams of pain. Several more loud bangs and scrapes issued out over the room, growing distant as though moving away before the comms fell silent for the last time.

Carter stood frozen in shock at what he had just heard. He knew those screams: they were screams of death.

"Car three . . . report in please," he muttered half-heartedly. The comms remained dead. He didn't bother calling them again.

He turned to face Harcourt slowly, sharing the numb expression on his face.

Hearing somebody . . . anybody die in that manner was never a nice experience. It was much the same as doing the deed yourself. There was no honour, no glory in it and the glint of survivor's guilt you always received in the aftermath was like a poisoned knife to the heart.

"Four dead, potentially another two as well, all for the sake of one thorn in the side," growled Carter.

He was furious. It was unacceptable and he knew it. That was four more servicemen who would never go back to their families, four more widows, and god knows how many kids left without a dad. The injustice of it all was overbearing.

"Patterson's good, but what do we do now?" Harcourt muttered.

"Call their commanding officer and inform him of their deaths. I'm going to need to see Fairfax. See what he wants us to do."

"And what do we do in the meantime?" Harcourt asked. "We don't even know if Patterson was involved in that crash."

"We carry on; we've got a job to do, so let's get it done."

Harcourt nodded and moved away.

We carry on. That's an easy thing to say, Carter told himself. Even then, he wasn't sure that he could.

*   *   *

Stacy rose with the sun, unable to sleep any longer. It had been a hard night for her, alone and worried to death. She had cried herself to sleep a mere three hours earlier. She looked in the mirror in her bathroom and only then did she recognise just how rough she looked. Her hazel eyes were blotchy and red from the crying.

She began to remember life with Danny before Carter had forced his way into their lives. Danny would wake up and put his arms around her slender body from behind, saying morning in his best cheesy grin before kissing her on the neck and shoulder, sending a shiver down her body in the process. He'd then proceed to the kitchen to cook them breakfast whilst Stacy spruced herself up and got herself ready for work as a secretary at a posh law firm in town.

Before she knew it, the air would be full of the rich smell of bacon and eggs and she would no doubt be blushing slightly as he made a general fuss over her.

Once a month, every month, he would surprise her with the biggest bunch of flowers he could afford, usually white roses, which were her favourite. Every now and again, she would catch him raving away to various songs on the radio, despite his best attempts to hide it from her. She usually laughed at him making a prat out of himself, before he'd realise he was being watched and grin like an idiot.

But that was all gone now; in the space of a week they had lost all reason to be happy and they were faced with an uncertain future, all hanging on whether or not Danny *could* escape from Carter. She began to shake slightly with the thought before pulling herself together with a shudder and busying herself with getting ready.

It felt weird being alone, she longed for Danny to lumber through the door now in his shorts and vest and take her in his arms as always.

It was the day of Steve's funeral, and Stacy was going as a sign of solidarity. Bill had mentioned the previous night that the others were still in the dark. The chances were that they wouldn't react well to Danny's disappearance, Jack especially. But they had to stay together; Stacy knew Danny was relying on them to remain strong and trust him as he trusted them.

There was a knock on the door as Stacy finished getting ready, and she hurried to the door to let Bill in. She gave him a watery smile as he entered, closing the door and following her into the kitchen.

Bill was dressed in a smart black suit; he hadn't bothered with the tie, preferring to keep the top button of his shirt undone. He looked sad to Stacy, as though the mere thought of the Funeral itself had hit him harder than Steve dying before his eyes had. He accepted Stacy's offer of a cup of tea solemnly and leaned against the kitchen side, staring off into space. Stacy didn't know what was going through his mind, and she was pretty sure she didn't want to know. She was under no illusions that, really, Bill wanted to be standing shoulder to shoulder with Danny and he wanted to take his revenge on Carter himself.

Despite everything, that last week had been extremely difficult on them, and now was the time they would have to put their best friend to rest for good. Stacy passed Bill his tea, who accepted it with a muted word of thanks. She looked at him and instantly recognised the look of sadness and grief in his eyes. She felt pretty taken aback by it, as she had never seen Bill that way before and it felt almost surreal. *Wrong.*

Bill always had been considered the toughest of the group, both physically and mentally and for him to show his emotions like this . . .

Stacy remembered how well Steve and Bill had got on together . . . *like a house on fire.*

They had acted like brothers.

"What time will Ade and Jack be over?" She asked quietly as she sipped at her coffee.

"Should be any time now," Bill replied.

He tore his eyes from the ceiling to look at her as he attempted to pull himself together.

Stacy nodded slightly and hesitated before asking her next question.

"They aren't going to react well to Danny leaving, are they?"

"If I'm honest, no," Bill told her, "and to be honest, I bloody wish Carter hadn't attacked Danny the night before Steve's . . ." His voice trailed off, unable to continue.

"I know what you mean, Bill. It's not right that he has to miss this. I just hope he's ok," she said quietly.

There was another knock on the door and Stacy moved to answer it; Bill was quickest, not taking any chances. He pulled the door open slightly, glancing through the crack before pulling it wide to allow Jack and Ade into the flat. Bill clapped them both on the back as they passed in their black suits and followed them into the kitchen where Stacy gave the two of them a quick hug before pouring them some tea.

"What was that all about?" Ade asked Bill as Stacy released him.

"Not taking any chances," he replied quickly.

"Why? And more to the point, where's Danny? I was looking forward to seeing his shocking dancing again," Jack smiled.

Ade grinned and Stacy giggled in spite of herself. Even Bill smiled slightly, pleased that at least somebody was attempting to remain upbeat.

"You wouldn't believe me if I told you," Bill muttered quietly.

"Try me," Jack shot back at him.

Bill didn't reply right away.

Would Jack believe him? Would Ade? It wasn't Danny's fault that he had been attacked by one of Carter's goons. Somebody he had begun to trust as an officer of the law. It had begun to feel like they were in a James Bond film. *Casino Royale eat your heart out,* Bill told himself.

"Last night, he was attacked," he began slowly.

"Attacked, who by?" Jack raised his eyebrows slightly.

"That copper, Greene. Turned out he worked for Carter and whatever his 'organisation' is," Bill replied. "Carter wants him dead."

Jack looked confused.

"I don't understand," he said.

"Look, those houses that went up last night, Danny was *involved* in it somehow. That's where he was attacked!"

"Hold on, Danny was there?" Ade interjected, "but that was a gas explosion for crying out loud."

The truth dawned on Jack there and then. He felt angry, betrayed.

"He went after Carter, didn't he," he growled. "He told me he wouldn't!"

Bill grew angry at Jacks reaction. Truthfully, he had no idea what had happened, only that Greene had tried to kill Danny and he and Carter had confronted each other soon after.

"Jack, calm DOWN!" he shouted, "Danny was not the one who started this and you know it."

"Where is he?" Ade asked over the top of Jack's cursing.

"I don't know, Carter threatened to kill Stacy, that's why he gone; to *protect* her from him."

Ade nodded in agreement; he didn't like the situation either, but perhaps if Danny had run then it *was* certainly with good reason. He turned on his heel, grabbing Jack and forcing him against the wall.

"Jack, this is not the time, you can argue with Danny if he survives this but until then we have a duty, as his *friends* to protect her-no LISTEN TO ME! Stacy is too important to us, and if Carter really wants her he's going to have to get through all of us first. We stand together; you above all people should know that!"

It took a while for Jack to calm himself down, and soon enough Ade let him go.

"I want to know everything you know Bill," Jack growled.

Bill raised his eyebrows. He doubted that Jack was really onside, but just wanted to know what had happened the previous night. Something had snapped inside him, and now all of a sudden Bill no longer trusted him. He thought long and hard about what he was about to say, paying no attention to anybody in the room as he lost himself in his thoughts. What would Danny do?

Would he tell him? Whether it was right or wrong of Jack to react in the manner he had, Danny would always remain a loyal friend to him no matter what happened. Bill fervently hoped that Jack would remember that fact because at the end of the day they were all in this together whether they liked it or not.

To hell with it, he told himself.

"It seems that Carter deems Danny a major threat to him and some big group he's a part of," Bill began slowly.

Jack listened intently as Bill continued

"Last night, Danny went to see Alex Stewart at his place 'cos he had claimed to have found out where Carter was.

"The reality was that it was a trap designed to isolate Danny so that Carter could take him out without any of us interfering"-

"Like Steve had, you mean?" Ade replied.

Bill nodded curtly.

"Anyway, Alex's partner, Greene had killed him prior to Danny's arrival and Danny had no choice but to fight to the death.

"All I really know from this point is that they fought, and Danny then shot Greene dead in self-defence. He then managed to scramble out before the gas main exploded and took out that row of houses."

Jack nodded his understanding, remaining dead quiet as he folded his arms across his chest tightly.

"I take it the man himself then showed up to finish the job?" he barked bitterly.

"Yep, and that leads us to the state we're in now. He gave Danny an ultimatum; leave the Park and stay away, or remain here and face losing Stacy."

Jack glanced at her as she let out an involuntary squeak of fear.

"*Now* do you understand why Danny's left?" Ade asked quietly.

Jack merely nodded. His throat was dry as he looked away from them and he began to feel a little bit stupid.

"Look mate, I'm not going to pretend that I'm any happier about this than you are, but I trust Danny, *with* my life," Ade continued. "We all know that if he could be here, he *would*. Wherever he is right now, I'm sure he's thinking of Steve and paying his respects in any way he can."

"The bigger picture," Jack agreed just as quietly.

*   *   *

8. The Funeral

Isn't it amazing how even the best laid plans can go wrong?

Here I am, in a country I know nothing about tearing its roads to shreds in an attempt to stay alive. I knew right away that Carter wasn't in any of those cars. He was safe and sound while his buddies did all the dirty work.

I saw my life flash before my eyes as the Almera flew through the air, and I told Stacy that I loved her before everything went black.

D anny had always been capable of looking after himself, and it was more than evident that it came with the territory.

He drew his jacket together and zipped it up to give him that extra little bit of warmth as he strode through the wet and windy streets of Leigh Park towards the old BP garage in the distance. He looked to his left as he passed the school and smiled as he laid eyes on the houses just across the Hermitage Stream. He of course knew the girl who lived in one of those terraced houses that curved sharply away from him like a crescent moon. It had been around three months since he had first met Stacy Ryan, even if that particular memory wasn't the happiest of such. He shuddered with the thought of what he had been forced to do on that cold evening even though he knew that it had been necessary at the time. There was no doubting that she was exceptionally beautiful, with warm hazel eyes that simply sparkled with life and brunette hair that fell in a silky curtain down past her shoulders that complimented her pale skin and slender body. She had a smile that would more or less blow Danny away every time he saw it . . .

He snapped his attention back to the rain sodden path before him as he felt the driving rain pounding into his face and quickened his pace as the rain grew heavier and reached the garage a few minutes later. He stepped quickly into the shop and flicked his hood back with his hand as he made his way down the right hand aisle and swept the rain from his face with a groan. He moved through the aisles, grabbing the small bits of shopping that he actually needed, before reaching the chilled drinks section and grabbing a can of Dr Pepper.

He checked his phone as he joined the queue to pay for the shopping and smiled at Ade's latest joke. He had to admit, it was a good one. He slipped the mobile back into his pocket as the counter became free. He quickly paid for his stuff and smiled at the shop girl as he picked up his carrier bag and left the shop. Danny threw his hood back over his head as he strode quickly back into the rain and grimaced as it began to drive into his face again.

The truth was that Danny didn't like the rain. He always had been more than content to sit indoors and hibernate until the weather cleared up. He was more of a sun-and-sea type, preferring the warmth and the feel of the sun on his face. He stepped across the forecourt quickly and began to retrace his steps back home to his tiny flat in The Warren.

He heard his name from behind him after a moment, and he recognised the Scottish accent without any problem. He turned to face Bill, his sandy hair instantly recognizable amongst the youthful looks he had been blessed with as he made to catch him up. Just behind him was Stacy, her hair slightly matted and stuck to her forehead as a result of the rain.

Something deep inside Danny fell at that moment as he remembered that they had been on a lunch date in town. It was more than apparent that Danny liked Stacy a lot, and it was often that his friends, especially Ade, would take the mickey out of him for it. Even though Danny paid no attention to the ribbings, he couldn't help but be drawn in by her. Everything from those warm hazel eyes to her soft ivory skin, it all attracted him to her like a moth to a flame. He often wondered whether she had noticed it or not. Of course he meant no ill of Bill or any other lads who were doubtlessly queuing for a chance to get with her, but for some reason he had always been incredibly protective towards her, and he had proved that fact on the very night they had met three months ago. His heart jumped a beat as she smiled at him and pulled him into a hug. He wrapped his own arms around her body and gave her a friendly squeeze before releasing her and returning the smile warmly.

"Where's my hug?" Bill chuckled playfully as he watched them.

Danny laughed and turned towards him, feigning a number of emotions as he pulled Bill into a bone cracking bear hug. Stacy laughed as they hugged each other.

"Good to see you again, ginger," Danny smiled.

"You too, you bloody menace you!" Bill replied. "And that's enough hugging, or do you want people to start talk?"

They released each other as they laughed; Danny shot Stacy a quick wink.

"How'd the date go? He asked them brightly.

"Yeah it was pretty cool," Bill smiled, "until this damn rain spoiled it anyway."

Stacy nodded her agreement with a slight smile.

"Typical English weather mate," Danny told him. "You must be wishing that your mum and dad had stayed in *bonny Scotland.*"

"Leave Scotland out of it," Bill grinned.

"Is this all you two do?" Stacy asked them as she chuckled.

"Of course it is," Danny beamed. "You could always help me as it's a barrel a laugh . . . although it doesn't take your fancy you could always help Ade annoy Steve, and those two are like an old married couple."

"I'll pass thanks," she replied with a grin.

Bill laughed silently at Danny's rejection and received a playful shove in return.

"You two are mad," Stacy giggled.

"Aye Stace we are, but I'm sure you wouldn't have it any other way," Bill replied.

"True," she conceded as she watched Danny crack open his can.

Her eyes lingered on his still form, following the shape of his body from head to toe before looking into his grey-blue eyes with a subtle longing that went completely unnoticed by both Bill and Danny. She tried to build up the courage to ask him the question that had constantly been on her mind as she watched his every move.

Stacy *did* like Bill; however she simply didn't see him in a romantic way the way she saw Danny. When she was with him, she felt safe and protected, and more importantly, she felt loved. Ever since that night three months ago she had felt desperately insecure about herself. And when she was hanging out with Danny and the others, those feelings disappeared. She knew that she loved him, and that was something she had been sure of since the moment he had emerged from the darkness to protect her on that night three months ago. It took all of her courage to sum up the will to ask him as she lost herself in his eyes once more.

"Bill, do you mind if I have some time alone with Danny?"

He nodded with a smile, and Danny handed him the keys to the flat and the bag of shopping without a word before shooting them a quick smile and striding away.

"So then, time alone with me eh?" Danny smiled lightly after a moment.

"Yeah, god only knows what I must be thinking," she sniggered.

Danny grinned at the joke as they began to walk slowly towards the group of houses that were just on their left hand side, crossing the stream as they wandered without any real need to hurry.

Stacy took Danny's hand, and it came as no real surprise to him. Since she had taken to spending time with him and the lads, he had long become used to her taking his hand and holding it as though it was some sort of talisman. And to be honest Danny didn't blame her, the events of that night three months ago had really shaken her, even more than he had originally realised at the time. Stacy never had been that confident about herself, so to have something like that happen to her would have done nothing but add to those insecurities. It was a well-known fact that she felt safer nowadays when Danny was nearby. He wasn't sure why that was the case, but he would protect and support her regardless of that fact.

He loved the feel of her soft skin against his own, like satin. And he smiled slightly as he saw her grinning in an almost triumphant way. Her eyes were alight and wide with happiness and she paid no attention at all to the drifting rain that surrounded the two of them as the ambled slowly up the road hand in hand.

"How did the date really go?" Danny asked softly after a moments quiet.

"It was fine," she replied with a smile, "but it just wasn't what I wanted if you know what I mean . . ."

"Oh? And what did you want?"

Stacy stopped and turned to look into Danny's eyes. She tightened her grip on his hand as she hesitated and was momentarily unsure what to say.

Danny smiled in encouragement and squeezed her hand in response.

"C'mon, you can tell me. Whatever it is I promise not to laugh."

"I wanted . . ." she took a deep breath and brought their hands up to rest against her heart, "I wanted you, Danny."

His jaw fell open as the shock hit him, and his eyes widened in surprise. What was she trying to say?

He felt her heart beating powerfully underneath his hand, a steady drumbeat that was nothing short of perfection. Danny glanced into those beautiful hazel eyes and he lost himself almost immediately. In that moment he no longer cared about anyone or anything. He had all he needed. And it was the breathtakingly beautiful girl in front of him.

"I love you Danny," she whispered.

It took him a moment to click on, and when her admission finally registered with him a mere fleeting second later his mouth began to slowly stretch into the warmest of smiles.

He couldn't believe that Stacy had in fact held the same feelings he had held for her. He felt nothing but happiness, pure unadulterated bliss as he pulled her close and leaned in to kiss her. She met him halfway and kissed him with a passion that Danny could never have anticipated. He pressed his hand to the small of her back to pull her closer and she responded with such force that they stumbled to the floor, landing on the grassy verge and paying no attention to the rain as they broke apart and laughed. Danny pulled her onto his lap as he sat up and she gasped quietly as she noticed his blue-grey eyes truly blazing with nothing but delight. He beamed at her and she returned the smile as he raised his hand to run his fingers softly through her hair.

"Just so you know," he murmured, "I've always loved you. You have no idea how long I've been waiting for you . . ."

She pressed a finger to his lips to silence him, before leaning in to kiss him for the second time . . .

That was when he woke up to a scene of utter devastation.

*   *   *

Now, if there was one thing Carter hated more than anything else in the world, it was *Boats*. He really could not stand them, always having that nagging, awkward feeling that the boat was so fragile it would sink at any moment without any hint of a warning.

As it stood, he was stuck as a foot passenger on a Red Funnel Ferry service to Cowes, Isle of Wight. He was half hour into the 60 minute voyage across the Solent and the sea was agitated and rough, pounding against the hull of the ferry and tossing it around like a ragdoll as though desperate to claim it for its collection of sunken vessels deep below the surface. He clutched the arms of his chair tightly as the ship pitched and rolled from side to side as it battled through the waves that assaulted it without mercy. Carter had to wonder just *how* the sailors coped with these conditions, and then thanked his lucky stars that he hadn't followed up on his decision to join the Navy all those years ago.

The voyage itself was necessary as his commander, General Fairfax had his residence on the island and that was where he ran the show. His boss was a bit of a dark legend within the services. Middle aged, he had a powerful presence about him. Carter remembered the strange bout of fear he had felt when he had first met Fairfax as a freelancer. He hadn't changed in the intermittent years. He truly was *the* boss, but only because every man and woman in the organisation was scared of attempting to rip the power he wielded from him. His plans however, were agreed on unanimously time and time again, and this one was their most ambitious yet.

In a James Bond film The Rogues would have been seen as the bad guys attempting to take over the world for whichever nefarious purpose they had cooked up, but this was reality and Carter knew that. Fairfax had had enough of the government's treachery towards its armed forces and now he sought revenge, a sentiment that was shared by everyone in the organisation. Carter already knew what Fairfax would want him to do with regards to Danny, but he wanted to hear it from the horse's mouth itself. He wondered why life couldn't just be simple, but couldn't find an answer as the ship pushed on determinedly.

*   *   *

At eleven, the hearse carrying Steve's coffin arrived and the funeral party all began to congregate outside Steve's father's house.

The undertakers, dressed in their traditional attire walked in front of the hearse sombrely as members of the public stopped and bowed their heads in respect, or removed their hats and for a moment the area fell silent. After a few minutes the hearse came to a stop in front of the assembled party and the undertaker turned to bow at the coffin. Behind the hearse were three black limousines that the undertakers had laid on for them. Their engines purred silently as they idled.

The party began to lay flowers and cards inside the hearse and Stacy began to move forward with a large bouquet of roses bearing Steve's name. She faltered as she grew nearer and wished almost desperately that Danny would suddenly appear at her side to guide her onwards. But he didn't come. She glanced back at Bill as the first few tears fell down to her cheeks. He nodded soberly and moved forward to assist her as he had agreed earlier. Jack threw his arm out to stop him, and with a slight smile he moved forward to help Stacy onwards. He put his arm around her shoulders to comfort her and took the bouquet from her to place carefully inside the hearse. He touched the polished wood of the coffin and bowed his head in thought.

"Sleep well, old friend," he muttered as he straightened up.

Bill gave them a watery smile as they fell back into line, whilst a stony faced Ade gave Jack a slap on the back.

Soon enough the procession was ready to leave and Stacy, Bill, Ade and Jack made their way to the second limo in line and were joined by two more people whom they had never met. The lead undertaker bowed to the coffin once more and then began the slow march to the end of the road. There he climbed into the hearse and the procession made their way through the streets towards their final destination.

*   *   *

Danny had felt the impact quite severely and he was certain that he had a small case of whiplash where his right shoulder was so stiff. He was searching the suburbs, keeping off the main roads and sticking to back alleys and minor roads. The blood that covered the side of his head had dried up, sticking to his skin like a layer of paste, giving him the impression of a Harvey Two-Face lookalike.

In the two hours that had passed he had made it six miles north of the area of Dunfermline where he'd smashed into several oncoming vehicles trying to stop the last of the Breras that had helped him wreck part of Edinburgh and cause several pile ups on the Forth Bridge. He was just thankful to be alive. The experience had taught him to be more cautious about himself, checking to make sure he wasn't being followed every few moments as he kept on moving.

He popped open the catch of an old wooden gate, entering a small back garden and ducking under the window of the newly built house in front of him. Slowly and carefully, he glanced inside to make sure no one was inside the house. Using the mangled bit of metal he'd ripped off the wrecked Almera, he dug it into the doorframe and heaved. After a minute, part of the wooden frame came away and Danny stumbled back with the force of it. The door shifted slightly, and Danny lashed out with his foot, aiming for the weakened area around the lock. It only took the one go as it shuddered on its hinges before swinging open and grabbed it to prevent it slamming against the back wall as he stepped inside. He moved quietly through the house, making sure nobody was home. Once he was satisfied, he relaxed slightly and strode into the bathroom to clean himself up. The dried blood came away slowly, and it remained sticky to the touch. When he was finished, he went into the master bedroom and checked the wardrobes. He was lucky, finding a set of clothes that were roughly his size. He ripped off his tattered and bloodied clothes, and changed instead to a sturdy pair of dark jeans, grey shirt and then nabbed the dark leather jacket from the coat stand in the corner of the room. He then switched his boots for a white pair of lace up trainers that fit his feet nicely.

When he was done he gathered up his old clothes, and moved down to the ornately decorated kitchen where he shoved the old gear into a black bag. He helped himself to some bread and butter, finally giving in to the hunger that he had battled for hours.

He stopped to think for a moment, checking the time and then bowed his head and fell silent for a minute. He remembered Steve and wished him a good sleep before thinking of Stacy and whether she was coping or not. He still had a fair distance to go before he reached his destination and prepared to leave, checking the old piece of paper in his hand to make sure he was going the correct way.

The sound of the lock in the front door down the hall clicked, and Danny heard the door swing open. He reacted quickly, grabbing his stuff and ducked out of the house. He didn't bother to stop to shut the gate, throwing the bag of clothes into the bushes and running for the woods that loomed ahead of him.

*   *   *

Carter looked relieved to be back on dry land as he left Cowes ferry port. He hated the town, full of hills and hundreds of boats that filled the River Medina time and time again. It was no wonder it had always been associated with Yacht races. He walked briskly into the town centre, blending into the crowd with consummate ease. He came to a halt outside a McDonald's drive thru and waited.

Fairfax was a very careful man, distrusting of everyone. He had set it up as a rendezvous point for the people in his inner circle should they wish to see him. Fairfax himself lived in a plush mansion on the outskirts of Ryde and had chosen the Isle of Wight to base himself simply because the resources of the authorities were limited on the island. Had they been discovered, Fairfax had a nice little buffer with which he could escape the island before any meaningful response could be made. Carter admired his prudence as a dark blue BMW pulled up alongside. He didn't waste time with the pleasantries as he clambered into the front passenger seat and settled down for the ride across the island.

*   *   *

It was a forty five minute trip to the crematorium, and as the procession gradually drew closer to their destination silence prevailed. Nobody spoke as the clouds deepened to a pewter grey colour. It was as though the planet itself was mourning.

Soon the procession completed its descent from the hill road and turned into the finely kept driveway of Portchester crematorium. The limousines pulled up one by one, its occupants taking their leave of the vehicles and gathering whilst the hearse bearing Steve's coffin came to a halt by the entrance to the chapel. The pall bearers, including Jack, Ade and Bill came forward now, hoisting the coffin onto their shoulders and carrying it slowly and carefully into the chapel.

As per Steve's wishes, The Goo-Goo Dolls' song, *Iris,* played in the background as the pall bearers entered, shortly followed by the rest of the party. The chapel was an ornately decorated room, awash with rich colours of crimson and cream that oozed warmth and created a real feeling of comfort. Stacy hung back slightly, unsure whether she could carry on as her rich hazel eyes remained locked on the coffin as it was lowered onto a marble podium at the front of the hall. She instinctively looked round her shoulder in the vain hope that Danny would be behind her, ready and willing to support her. When he didn't appear before her expectant eyes, she shivered as that desperate feeling of loneliness hit her like a ten ton anvil. Somehow, without really knowing how she had done it, she pulled herself together and regained her composure before taking a seat on one of the oak pews that furnished the room. Bill, Ade and Jack joined her after a few minutes, each of them looking as though they were about to crack. They sat in silence as the chapel continued to fill up. Soon enough the service began, and the reverend said his piece, before the congregation rose to sing the first of the hymns. The trio led the singing, showing the solidarity that Bill had asked of them, solidarity and loyalty towards their fallen friend.

The reverend then invited Bill forward for the analogy. He walked slowly, purposefully to the front and faced them with an ashen faced expression. He took a moment to compose himself, and then began to speak.

"Some say the world will end in fire, some say in ice.

From what I've tasted of desire I hold with those who favour fire.

But if it had to perish twice, I think I know enough of hate to say that for destruction ice is also great and would suffice.

"I believed this once, as did Steve. It seems to me that this world has a knack for taking all of the people we love from us," Bill paused as he composed himself once more.

"Steve was truthfully one of the greatest men I've had the pleasure to know. He was a loyal friend, fiercely so. He was also the consummate gentleman who possessed a heart of gold. He was never afraid to put his life on the line for us, always the one who would take one for the team. He was the one who kept us going, despite being a born worrier. We used to take the mick out of him for it, but he would always hit back with a light-hearted smile and that sarcastic manner that we knew and loved him for."

Bills voice broke as he spoke and the first of the tears began to fall from his eyes. He fought his emotions, attempting to keep himself controlled as he continued in a shaky voice.

"Steve was like a brother to me. He shouldn't have been taken from us like this, it's *wrong*. His memory will always live on, in all of us. Never forget him, as he never forgot us. Sleep well, old friend."

Bill strode back to his seat as the congregation applauded him.

Next it was Steve's fathers turn to speak, and it took a couple of tries before he was able to summon up the courage, such was his grief for his loss. While he spoke about Steve's life, nobody talked. Everybody showed an overwhelming amount of respect towards each other. They stood to sing the next hymn, united in grief and united as they celebrated Steve's life. Then the service ended and everybody in the room remained on their feet in a mark of respect as the crimson curtains closed and blocked the coffin from view. The priest said his piece as *Iris* began to play for the second time and the congregation began to file slowly out of the chapel and into the gardens of remembrance.

*   *   *

General Thomas Fairfax was an extravagant man and he knew it. Everything from the crisp, personally tailored clothes down to the beautifully designed works of art that adorned the wood panelled walls of the old mansion he had owned for the last decade or so.

In the impressive drawing room where he would spend his evenings in front of a roaring fire and his head in a good book, lay several medals for bravery and a five year old MBE on the rich oak mantelpiece. Born into a rich upper class family in 1955, the plush lifestyle had always been something he had *inherited*. It had been all he had known right from the day he had been born . . . his *birth right*, you could say.

He shifted in his armchair, not bothering to rip his eyes from *War and Peace* as he settled back into the comfortable leather chair. The red velvet curtains lay open to expose the windows as light flooded into the room from the south.

Fairfax wasn't a patient man, and as he checked the Omega watch on his left wrist, he exhaled heavily. He expected Carter at any moment and to be brutally honest; he was looking forward to discussing his little problem regarding Danny Patterson. It was no surprise that Carter was so deeply interested in him, after all it was Carter's own fault that the young man had been left without a father in the first place. Why he wanted the truth kept from him was understandable, if perhaps a little stupid. Was Danny Patterson really so much of a threat to him?

Fairfax remained unconcerned as he checked his watch for the second time and continued to ponder.

*   *   *

The rain began to fall, slowly at first, before suddenly getting heavier and there was quite a chill in the air as Danny battled into the hills north of Dunfermline. The muscles in his legs groaned in protest as he struggled against the terrain and his clothes and were sopping wet as the rain continued mercilessly. His hair lay plastered to his forehead as the cold water began to freeze him and he wished he was back with Stacy once again.

He had had it with the whole good guy-bad guy thing between him and Carter. Thanks to him, Danny was climbing a Scottish mountain trying to find shelter in a country that was completely alien to him, despite the heritage gained from his Dad.

What is the point? Danny asked himself angrily. He believed now that he would actually have been better off back in Leigh Park, taking his chances; at least that way if he *was* to die he would be with Stacy, in his hometown. That was how he wanted it to be . . .

Danny shrugged the thought from his mind as he continued his battle against both the elements and the hill side. It took another ten minutes or so before the terrain levelled out and his feet found flat ground one more. He stopped, bent double as he caught his breath, inhaling and exhaling in long drawn out breaths and when he straightened up a few minutes later he glanced at his soaked, filthy clothes and groaned slightly. He turned around to admire the view from the summit, and his jaw dropped in surprise.

And a beautiful view it was too; the hill towered over the town below; and further on was the Firth of Forth and the famous bridges that spanned it. Beyond that and right at the very limit of his vision lay the City of Edinburgh.

Danny whistled in admiration as he watched the rain fall in bands across the land in front of him. He had heard people talk about Scotland's natural beauty on several occasions throughout the years, but now was the first time he had experienced it for himself; he only wished it had been under happier circumstances.

It was almost saddening as Danny tore his eyes from the scene before him. But he had something that needed to be done and he could ill afford to hang around in the pouring rain all day. He turned to face the thick Forrest behind him and began to head into its depths. When Danny emerged into the clearing half an hour later, he was faintly surprised to find the large wooden cabin sitting there as though it was a part of the landscape. A dirt driveway that was soaking up the rain water quite nicely stretched from the porch, and a concrete garage the seemed at odds with the woods around it lay just off to the left. Danny felt a surge of pride, for the cabins owner was an extremely old friend of the family. He moved quietly over to the porch, reaching out and knocking the door sharply.

Soon enough the door opened to reveal a lanky, middle aged man with a muscular build that defied his height. His jaw was deep set and rigid, and had a mop of red hair that gave the impression of a burning fire on top of his head. His rich brown eyes stared at Danny with surreal disbelief.

"Hello Paul," Danny smiled, "it's good to see you again."

*   *   *

In the days leading up to the service, it had been agreed that the ashes should be released into the Solent at Hayling by both family and close friends; namely Steve's father and Ade, Bill, Danny, Jack and Stacy. They met outside of the chapel as the first drops of rain began to fall and shook hands with the lads and took Stacy's hand and kissed it respectfully.

"Thanks for coming guys, I appreciate it," Jim told them quietly.

"It's no problem Jim, I'm just glad we got through it in one piece," Ade replied with a slight smile.

James 'Jim' Tavistock was getting old. His once-brown hair was turning a silvery grey colour and was balding around the crown. He was practically the spitting image of his son; tall and powerfully built with what would have been classed as extremely good looks back in the sixties. He had never once believed that it would be him burying his son, instead of his son burying him. Steve had been his oldest son, and he had loved him as such. He doubted he would ever get over the grief.

"Yes, I can imagine it was hard for you all, after all you were all there when . . ."

"It is, believe me," Jack cut in quickly as soon as Jim faltered.

Jim nodded in agreement as his emotions got the better of him.

Stacy moved forward to console him, giving his shoulder a squeeze.

"We're going to do it tonight, we'll understand if you don't want to join us."

"No, no I'll be there. It's our last chance to say goodbye after all," Jim told her quietly.

Stacy gave him an encouraging smile as they began to walk around through the gardens of remembrance.

"You never said . . . where's Danny?"

Stacy's heart skipped a beat and she glanced quickly over to Bill, a gesture that Jim caught immediately.

"Stacy, please, what's going on? I think I deserve to know what's happening."

"Steve's killer went after Danny last night. He was lucky to get out alive," Bill told him quietly.

"Where is he now?"

Bill shrugged. "We don't know. Carter threatened to kill Stacy if he didn't leave."

"So he left to protect her, yes?" Jim asked with a great deal of concern in his voice.

"Yes," Stacy whimpered.

Jim shook his head in disbelief as they came to a halt. "I can't believe this is happening. What's Danny done to deserve being chased by a killer?"

"Danny thought that there was an ulterior motive, something that connects them. The only thing we know is that it wasn't gang related."

"That's comforting," Jim growled. "The news said this morning that he had killed the officers investigating and that he's the subject of a massive manhunt."

"He didn't," Stacy shrieked heatedly, "Greene tried to kill *him*!"

"That's going to change things," Bill groaned.

"Yeah, what's the betting Carter put that one out?" Ade interjected.

"I'm guessing Danny has no idea then?" Jim asked.

"Not about the police physically chasing him, no," Bill replied quietly after a moment's silence. If what Jim was saying was true, things had just got a hell of a lot harder for Danny . . . wherever he was.

Bill was determined to help him in whatever way possible, but without a way to contact him they were as good as cut off. Bill swore under his breath as the ire and frustration hit him. Only Stacy noticed.

9. The Truth Revealed

I never believed that it was possible, even for a moment. Was this the reason why Carter was so obsessed with me? The reason we seemed so inexplicably linked?

I knew what The Rogues were; who they were. The thought of what they were planning disgusted me as I looked my dad's best friend in the eye and I was thankful that I finally knew the truth.

Somebody once said that you could either die a hero or live long enough to see yourself become a villain. I knew what I'd prefer.

" **W**hat the hell are you doing up here Danny?" Paul Rogers shouted from his kitchen as he bustled about making tea impatiently.

"I was in the neighbourhood . . . so I thought I'd come and see you," Danny replied brightly.

"In the neighbourhood," Paul scoffed, "you made a right bloody mess down in town earlier so don't give me the social call crap."

"You heard about that huh?" Danny replied sheepishly as Paul re-entered the front room with two steaming mugs of tea.

Paul had lived amongst the Scottish wilderness for almost half a decade. Originally a Sussex lad, he had grown up in Chichester before running away aged sixteen to become a boy soldier, eventually joining the Para's. In the years that followed he progressed through the ranks and passed the SAS selection program in 1988. From that point onwards he had been forced to grow more secretive about his work, and in January 1990 he was seconded to The Increment—the only unit that the government denied all knowledge of. This 'ghost' unit was the best of the best, comprised mainly of members of the SAS and the SBS and tasked with the tasks that not even MI5 or the SIS (MI6) would dirty their hands with. Not long after, Paul had been picked to go on the mission to Iraq that had gone so disastrously wrong. At the time, he had been gutted to have picked up a hernia whilst out on his morning run and had wished his friends well in the pub the night before they were due to leave. By the end of that week, his opinion had changed drastically and as a result he had lost several great friends as a result, including Colin Patterson.

Paul knew that Danny had always wondered what had happened to his father, but as a result of the government's disavowing of the unit and the subsequent Official Secrets Act being shoved down both Paul's and Danny's mother's throats, they weren't able to tell him.

Even after all this time Paul still felt as though he had let Danny down, thereby insulting his old friend's memory.

"Of course I did Danny, did you really think that a car crash would escape attention?"

Danny shrugged his shoulders before taking the mug of tea offered to him and taking a sip. The hot liquid burned the back of his throat as it went down, but it tasted good nonetheless. Danny immediately felt his body react to the warmth inside him and he began to warm up once more.

"Seemed like a good idea at the time," he replied coolly.

"Just like your old man," Paul growled. "And you still haven't told me why you're up here."

"You wouldn't believe me if I told you."

"I may be getting on a bit, but I'm not stupid Danny. I'm here to help, remember?"

Of course, Paul was right. He'd been there since the beginning, helping him and his mother. He had been one of the few people he had actually trusted back in his youth. Danny considered telling him; after all if anyone could help him, then it would certainly be Paul Rogers.

"Ok, if you want to know, you'll need to know the whole story as well," Danny told him quietly as he sat in one of the armchairs by the open fire.

"Yes," Paul replied simply as he joined him in the other armchair.

"A few days ago, a very good friend of mine was murdered by somebody called Carter."

"Alistair Carter? Was that his name?"

Danny shook his head. "I dunno, tall fella, around half a head taller than me. He's got a real penchant for suits."

"That sounds like him," Paul grunted.

"This Carter guy basically turned up out of nowhere and pulled a gun on my friend Jack. Then Steve threw himself in the way and took the bullets instead.

"I went for Carter, and I had him, but then Stacy got caught up in it and he managed to get away. We lost Steve on the way into the hospital."

"I'm sorry to hear that," Paul told Danny quietly. "So, what happened to force you up here?"

Danny settled himself back into his chair and eyed Paul apprehensively. He wasn't a naturally suspicious person, and he wasn't paranoid either. So why were his senses all screaming out to him that Paul; the closest thing he'd had to a father . . . was hiding something?

Then again, he'd had that feeling for years; almost as though he was keeping something from him deliberately, which in turn led to the obvious questions: what was he hiding? And *could* he be trusted?

"I went after Carter. We thought it was an Eastleigh attack at the time."

Paul nodded without smiling. He knew all the stories about the old rivalry and had heard about the countless bloody conflicts that had shaped the south coast over the years. He had once heard Colin talking about the battles when they were in the unit together, even going so far as to say that they would win the impending Gulf War in days if they sent the old gangs out to fight instead.

"Did you find him?" Paul asked in a concerned voice.

Danny shook his head. "He found me . . . well led me into a trap more like. The officers investigating Steve's murder; DC Alex Stewart and DCI David Greene are both dead as a result.

"Greene betrayed everyone. It turned out that he was actually working for Carter. He killed Alex and his wife last night and sent me a message from his phone. My curiosity got the better of me and I showed up like a good little boy."

Paul didn't move. He continued to gaze at Danny without betraying any hint of emotion as he listened.

"Anyway," Danny continued earnestly. "He turned his gun on me when I found the bodies and the next thing I know he's rabbiting on about how *the country will never be the same again in a couple of days' time*. What do you think that means?"

"I'm not sure . . ."

Danny did a double take as Paul's voice trailed off. Did he really know something?

Paul didn't miss it and sat up swiftly.

"Danny?" he asked quietly.

"There's something you're not telling me, isn't there?" Danny demanded.

Paul didn't answer, and it seemed as though he was making a decision . . . or wrestling with his conscience.

He put his head in his hands with a groan and cursed angrily.

"Paul, for god sake you're killing me here. If there's something you know I need to know as well!"

"Finish your story, and then I'll tell you everything." He growled through his hands, muffling his voice slightly.

Danny nodded and continued his story without out taking his eyes off of Pauls frozen form.

*   *   *

"So Alistair, it seems you have a bit of a problem," said Fairfax as he offered Carter one of the seats opposite him.

"That would be an understatement sir," Carter grimaced as he sat down opposite his commander.

It was Carter's second visit to the mansion, and he was still taken aback by the sheer size of it. Even with Fairfax himself and his small private army there was still enough space to shove a company or two into the spare rooms. *The man even has an armoury in the east wing,* Carter told himself in astonishment-a fact only pointed out to him by Harcourt a week earlier.

"Tell me about Mr Patterson."

"Well he's just like you explained to me with regards to his local area; tough, loyal and bloody stubborn-just like his old man.

"When I made the hit on Jack Harper he attacked me. He's quite a good little fighter, if a bit reckless."

"I met Colin just before the unit left for Iraq, and that was the exact opinion I got from him. Sounds like they're two peas in a pod," Fairfax replied with a nod.

"He doesn't know that it was my fault his dad is six foot under."

"And you're worried that he'll find out?"

"Wouldn't you be?" Carter growled irately.

He regretted his outburst right away. He was out of line and he knew it. Carter supposed that the memory of his darkest hour had been re-awakened tenfold by Danny's sudden appearance. He had known that Colin was a father and he could remember him talking about his young family to his mates on the Hercules C150 over to the Middle East a mere 48 hours before . . .

Carter shook the thought from his mind as he saw the faces of the seven soldiers who hadn't made it home.

"Would you like something to drink, Alistair?"

"Please," Carter replied with a nod

Fairfax rose from his chair and strode to the small bar behind Carter.

"You *were* out of line there; however I'll overlook it because I understand that young Danny has irritated you."

He pulled two ornate glasses from the cupboard and poured a generous amount of Whiskey into the glasses.

"I apologise sir, it's been a tough twenty four hours for me, as you already know."

"Yes, Ice?"

Carter nodded and rose to meet Fairfax at the bar and accepted his glass with muted thanks.

"Right, explain what actually happened in Scotland this morning," Fairfax said quietly

"In a nutshell, four men are dead and another two are unaccounted for; Gretna tracked Danny up through Lothian and into Edinburgh. He spotted them just as they were ready to make their move and he went north to try to shake them off," Carter told him. "The chase came to an abrupt end in Dunfermline, and from what I've heard from the local cell Danny's car and our lad's car were both totalled."

"Was Patterson recovered?"

Carter shook his head. "No sign of him. It doesn't surprise me."

"So you certainly believe that Danny Patterson is a threat?"

"Yes sir."

Fairfax eyed Carter *extremely* carefully, as though he was judging his credibility. Carter returned the look as he leaned against the bar.

"Ok," Fairfax began slowly as he took a sip of his drink. "I'm going to authorise a full alert and a capture-or-kill order on Patterson as priority number one. Agreed?"

"Yes sir," Carter replied with a nod.

"And whilst I'm doing that: I want you, and *only* you, to put your energy into locating him. With a bit of luck you can claim victory in your little game before one of my happy go lucky Privates find him. Do we have a deal?

"I'll have every resource at my disposal?" Carter asked.

Fairfax gave him a slight nod.

"Thank you sir, we have a deal."

Carter smiled slightly and drained his glass. He set it down and made to leave, before Fairfax called him back.

"Bear in mind Alistair, our main strike begins in two days. That's all the time I will give you."

"Sir," Carter nodded and gave him a swift salute before turning on his heels and strode for the exit.

*   *   *

Paul had been pacing anxiously around the room for a few minutes now, and Danny was growing increasingly irritated as he watched him.

It was without a doubt a true fact that Paul; having been a member of The Increment, knew just what was happening . . .

Danny had been shocked to discover just moments ago, that Carter knew both Paul and his father and that they had all been a part of the same unit that the government denied all knowledge of, and that reputably didn't even exist.

Danny saw the worry etched on Paul's face alongside another emotion . . . *Uncertainty?*

If Paul is worried then should I be as well? Danny asked himself.

Even then he knew that there was no way to answer that question until Paul explained exactly *what* he knew.

"Paul, do me a favour and stop holding out on me," he half shouted after a few moments.

Paul began grumbling to himself, catching occasional curses and mutterings about the Official Secrets Act. After a moment he seemed to reach a decision and stopped his pacing.

"Back in the day there was a lot of rumours flying about the intelligence services about a group of squaddies led by a man named Thomas Fairfax who were planning to strike back at the government over their *mistreatment* of ex forces personnel and for generally messing up the country.

"Rumour had it that they wanted to take over and bring Britain back to her rightful position in the world. *Britannia rules the waves.*"

"What did they do about it?" Danny grimaced.

"Nothing, Thames House believed that it didn't warrant any monitoring. Both SIS and MI5 sat back and concentrated on what would soon become the Gulf War and combating the IRA."

"What about you? Did you believe the rumours?"

Paul didn't answer right away. He moved slowly and collapsed back into his armchair, looking exhausted as he put his head back in his hands.

"Perhaps," he muttered, "I certainly believed it was possible with enough manpower. To be honest, I didn't even know The Increment existed until SIS seconded me. When that happens you tend to believe any rumour, no matter how small."

"Anything you know about them would help me, Paul." Danny murmured quietly.

Paul stared at the fire before replying. "As I said, there were rumours . . . no, more like whispers, that a splinter cell of The Increment were planning to attempt some sort of coup d'état against the British government in revenge for its insulting of the servicemen of her majesty's armed forces."

"But surely they would have been crushed by those loyal to queen and country?"

"That's what I thought," Paul agreed with a nod. "But what you've told me worried me; everything sounds like an Increment led operation. And if they've called themselves "The Rogues", that could well mean they plan to give it a real shot."

"What's with the name?" Danny asked quietly.

"It was the nickname of mine and your dad's old unit in The Increment. The same unit Alistair Carter was a member of."

Danny froze in disbelief. In that instant a dozen different emotions crossed his face; shock turned to anger, anger turned to betrayal. He turned slowly to glare at the man who had known and fought alongside his enemy and before he knew it he was on his feet, his hands balled up into fists so tight that the knuckles seemed to strain against the skin. In his mind, Danny blamed Paul for all of this, simply knowing Carter was betrayal enough. It took a while to clear his head of his thoughts and by that time it was already far too late. Paul had noticed.

"Danny, sit down. It's time you knew what actually happened to Colin.

Danny glared back at Paul at first before doing as he was told.

"Whatever happened to him has some relevance to me, doesn't it?" he growled.

Paul nodded and took a deep breath as he looked right into Danny's eyes. He saw the anger there immediately, holding pride of place against what seemed to be half a dozen other emotions that were waging a pitched battle for control over his mind. Amongst the raging inferno he recognised the most potent emotion of all; and that was fear. Paul had no doubts in his mind that Danny was scared and he had to admit, he was doing a pretty good job of hiding it. He could see that Danny had accepted the fact of his own mortality and it terrified him . . .

"Carter was involved, wasn't he?" Danny interrupted just as Paul opened his mouth to speak. His jaw locked shut as he stared wide eyed at him.

"How . . . ?" Paul stuttered after a second

"The way he looked at me, there was *something* there that I couldn't figure out. It was like he was scared of me."

"It's probably because he sees what I see. Danny, you have always been the absolute spitting image of your father and right now you look exactly like Colin just before he was killed.

"I'm afraid I don't know the full details regarding your father's death, only that the mission went sour and Colin was killed because Carter bottled it in combat."

"Did mum . . . ?" Danny's throat was dry as he spoke and he couldn't bring himself to finish.

"Yeah the MOD told her . . . just after they forced us to sign the Official Secrets Act," Paul spat angrily.

Danny froze for the second time as a new, stronger bout of anger set in. In his mind he tried to make sense of it all, to try to find an answer. None came.

However, Danny could understand Pauls dislike for the authorities who had forced a gag order on a grieving widow. Why had there been such a need to cover up a failed military operation?

"Well why was all the secrecy needed? I don't get it," he asked after a minute of silence.

Paul shifted in his seat, suddenly looking defensive as he tore his eyes from Danny's still form.

"I can't tell you why. You'll discover the reason in your own time. Part of me wonders if Carter will tell you himself."

Danny leaned forward, hesitating slightly, "What makes you say that?"

"Danny I'm not an idiot, I can see what you're planning. Why the hell else would you be *here*?"

"I'm not going to fight him," Danny chuckled. "I'm going to get back down to get Stacy from Havant, and then who knows. The sky's the limit."

"Don't give me that," snorted Paul.

"I'm serious."

Paul shook his head, unable to believe what he was hearing. Danny, he knew, was no coward. But he also knew that he could never hope to win an argument with him. The stubbornness that lay within Danny ran in the family after all . . .

Just like his old man, Paul groaned to himself.

"Okay, whatever you say," he muttered as he held his hands up to admit defeat. "But, I'm not letting you jump out of the frying pan and into the fire without a hope in hell of physically *surviving."*

Danny's curiosity peaked as Paul beckoned for him to follow as he rose from his chair. He felt calm as he followed him out of the house and into the rain.

10. Playing Poker, with Life as the Currency

I should have known that Carter wouldn't have kept his word the very second I turned my back on him.

I've been running from responsibility my entire life; faster than ever before it seemed. I was time I stopped and stood my ground. I had once sworn to protect the people I loved on pain of death and it was about time I honoured that oath. I wasn't afraid of death and as long as I still had a cause to fight for I would gladly trade my life for their safety.

Hayling Island was one of those places where you would always be pleasantly surprised to find an inhabited area. It was a tiny thing, shaped like an upside down wonky T and was connected to the mainland by a single road bridge at Langstone yet despite its size it was home to a few holiday parks and caravan sites.

Since they had left the service, the car containing Jim, Stacy and the three lads had an extremely subdued atmosphere as it wound its way through the narrow roads to the Island's southernmost point. The rain grew harder as they drew nearer to their destination and the wind, pushing gale force at times, battered the old BMW 3 Series as though it was a mere toy at times. When they eventually arrived at the seafront the wind was blowing a gale, stirring up the dark grey sea that kicked up onto the beach in furious waves.

Jim brought the car to a halt in the tiny car park near the seawall that struggled to hold back the angry waves. He turned to face his passengers with a look of both resignation and acceptance.

"Ready?"

"Yeah," Stacy nodded and knew immediately that she spoke for everyone in the car.

They made no noise as they clambered out of the car and stepped into the rain. It drove into their faces and soaked into their clothes; their hair grew into a multitude of dishevelled states and stuck to their foreheads in places as they walked towards the sea wall. The sea occasionally kicked up over the old flood defences, sending spray a good fifteen feet into the air before crashing down over the path.

Bill considered Stacy momentarily before deciding to gesture for her to stay back. She hesitated as Jim and the others stopped and in the same instant, more spray kicked up over the wall, showering them with the dull grey sea water and Stacy decided that maybe it was a good idea to stay back after all. She shivered as the cold got to her and Bill looked back at her, before handing the small urn to Ade and strode back to put his arm around her to keep her warm. They stood there together and watched silently as Ade cast Steve's ashes slowly into the wind.

"Danny's going to get through this, Stacy. You wait and see."

"I know he will. I believe in him," she replied. "One day this'll be over and we'll be able to finally settle down."

"I'm sure you will," Bill smiled. "Danny said you were talking about starting a family?"

Stacy nodded slightly. In the days before Steve's murder, Stacy and Danny had of course talked extensively about starting a family of their own. It was one of the only things they wanted from life. Stacy dreamed of that future. A full and satisfying life with Danny was all she would ever wish for, because that was all she wanted.

"I can't imagine Danny as a father for some reason," Bill told her quietly. "It's probably because I've always known him as the light-hearted, rebellious type."

"I can," she breathed. "He's more than capable of protecting them, loving them and we'd give them the best possible start in life."

"Well once all this agro with Carter's blown over, you two will be able to have that quiet life you've always dreamed of."

"If Danny survives, right?" she muttered quietly.

It was the only thing on her mind, her constant companion because of the fear she felt. When it's someone you love doing all of the fighting, you tend to get those kinds of rash ideas.

Of course, Stacy knew perfectly well that Danny was capable of looking after himself, as he had demonstrated on the night they had met. Every now and again, she would look back on those events with nothing but horror during her nightmares, however when her subconscious mind played on her fears at night, the dream took an entirely different approach, she would see *that man* coming after her, and then out of nowhere, Danny would appear just in time to intervene.

But the difference was that he wouldn't win the resulting fight, and it had been all too often that when she awoke from her nightmares, Danny was there waiting to take her into her arms and reassure her. Danny Patterson was the bravest man Stacy knew, and she was thankful that it was him who would take her gladly into his arms to comfort her. She wished he was here now to pull her close, where she could find peace and sanctuary in his arms. They were the only times she ever felt truly *safe*.

"Come on Stace, you know as well as I do he'll be ok. He'll be back for you soon enough."

"It just doesn't feel right without him. I'm looking round every corner thinking that Carter's there waiting for me."

Bill turned and pulled her into a hug as she began to panic again. It felt wrong, having to console his best friend's girl like this, but he had no other choice.

"We won't let him get anywhere near you. And neither will Danny," he murmured assertively. "Come on, you've got to be strong for him now. As long as he has you, he'll beat anyone and anything, and you alone know that to be true."

Stacy leaned herself into the hug, and Bill knew that she was desperately trying to find the security in his arms that she always found in Danny's. He released her as the others moved towards them; they had finished casting the ashes into the sea. They were drenched from the sea spray and said nothing as they passed on the way back to the car.

Bill smiled weakly as they passed before beckoning for Stacy to lead the way back to the car. He looked out to the sea, where a lone Wightlink Ferry battled its way indomitably through the waves towards the safety of the harbour. He wondered to himself if it was just the calm before the storm. It was too quiet, and he felt edgy as he turned back to clamber into the car with the others.

*   *   *

Carter felt visibly sick as the ferry tossed and turned with the waves and he struggled to understand just how this weather had appeared so quickly. The ferry pitched and rolled another twenty degrees as the waves slammed furiously and insistently into the hull. An alarm issued from somewhere down on the vehicle storage ramps as the spray kicked up over the sides. In the corner, a young boy was screaming that he didn't like what was happening, and quite frankly Carter didn't blame him. He looked into his mother's stony eyes and it was apparent that the boy had inherited it from her.

Carter had a plan for when he finally managed to plant his feet on dry land once more, and that involved a stiff drink before heading back to where it had all started. He had unfinished business.

*   *   *

Danny looked around the second of Paul's log cabins with an expression of absolute shock. On the furthest wall lays racks of pistols and a couple of semi-automatic machine guns and below were two tables worth of ammunition and spare parts. It was like a scene from the video game *Hitman*. Did Paul even have a licence for these?

Danny shook his head in disbelief as he moved towards them and began to recognise the various makes and models; Walther, Glock, Beretta and even the Browning Hi-Power from the Chris Ryan books he had read over the years . . .

In the far corner was a makeshift range with cardboard cut outs for targets and Danny glanced back at it, wondering just why Paul had brought him here.

"Where the hell did you get all this stuff?" he asked faintly.

"I can't tell you. Not even the government knows that I've got all this stuff," Paul replied humourlessly as he started grabbing guns and loaded clips of bullets into their respective housings. He checked the safety on each weapon before laying them at Danny's feet.

"Full of surprises, aren't you?" Danny replied in an assertive voice.

Paul nodded quietly as he checked the final gun, before holding it out for him to take.

Danny eyed it carefully, as though it was a time bomb ready to go off at any second.

"As you said, I'm full of surprises," Paul told him without smiling. "This is the Browning Hi-Power. I'm not going to let you go back without being able to defend yourself, so I think I'd better teach you how to use this thing if the situation arises."

"I've already told you I'm not going back to fight him, Paul."

"Well he's not going to stop looking for you Danny, and when he finds you he *won't* be alone, and he *won't* be unarmed.

"You say you want to protect that girl of yours? *This* is the only way you can do it."

Danny glared angrily at him as he took the Browning from him. The steel felt cold and raw in his hands and as he looked down at it he wrapped his forefinger instinctively around the trigger. He knew how to fire a gun, and that thought still scared him.

"Right, before you step up to the plate you need to understand something. This pistol is of a single action design so you can't simply load, aim and fire. Before you fire, make damn sure that the hammer is thumbed back to cock it and load the first round into the chamber. Once the hammer's cocked it'll be ready to fire."

Danny listened in spite of himself, even if he knew he wouldn't need the *training*.

He followed Paul's instructions anyway, as he checked to ensure the hammer was cocked and made ready for firing. He stepped up to the firing plate; effectively just a strip of white tape that marked a fifteen metre distance between him and the targets on the range. He flicked off the safety and brought the gun up in his hand before resting his finger on the side of the trigger guard. He turned his body to the side slightly and spread his legs slightly apart for better balance.

Paul looked on as Danny did so and was immediately impressed by his preparations.

"I can see you weren't kidding about last night," he said quietly as he strode closer. "Now this pistol is a military model so the hammer won't snap at the web between the forefinger and the thumb. The magazine is a thirteen round clip; one round in the chamber and twelve in the magazine.

"When I say, I want you to squeeze the trigger, not pull it. I want you to fire three shots at the targets, ok?"

"Whatever you say," Danny replied. He moved the weapon slightly, bringing the first cardboard target into his sights. His arm was steady as he waited.

"Fire," Paul ordered quietly as he stepped back.

Danny took his time, bringing his right palm up to support his shooting arm before squeezing back slightly on the trigger three times. All three rounds exploded out of the gun within half a second of each other and slammed into the targets on the range. The noise was deafening as it fired and the noise rang in his ears as he flicked the safety and lowered the weapon.

He turned to Paul, who stared wide eyed at Danny whilst his right forefinger stroked the top of his lip. He hesitated for a moment before dropping his hand and strode across to check the ragged holes the bullets had ripped in the cardboard. When he had finished his inspection he wheeled around to look at Danny in amazement.

In all his years in the military, Paul had never seen a person shoot *that* well, especially a twenty year old. It was incredible.

"How the hell did you do that?" he asked in a feeble voice.

"I aimed this thing and fired it," Danny replied as he strode towards the targets for a closer look. "Are you afraid that I'm a better shot than you or something?"

"You got *three* headshots Danny; there are only two people I know who can shoot as well as that."

"And they are?"

"Both your dad and Alistair Carter were probably the best shooters around."

Danny feigned hearing loss as the anger he felt towards Carter reared its head once more. Carter was everywhere he turned.

"I'd still love to know where you learned to shoot so well," Paul challenged.

Danny shrugged nonchalantly. The truth was that he didn't know. The previous night had been the first time he had ever fired a live weapon.

"I'll let you know when I've figured it out," he murmured.

He laughed slightly and then turned to walk back to the firing plate.

Paul moved out of the line of fire as Danny raised the gun once more and opened fire.

*   *   *

Bill and Stacy said their goodbyes to the others in hushed voices before they climbed out of the car and ran for the cover of the tower block as the rain poured to the ground with a renewed ferocity. The torrential downpour had refused to cease like a stubborn child refusing to play nice and the drains began to lose the battle against the water that fell determinedly from the skies in huge sweeping curtains.

By the time Stacy and Bill had managed to get inside the warm shelter of the tower block in which their respective flats were located they were completely soaked to the skin and freezing cold. Nevertheless, Bill escorted her up to the fourth floor flat she shared with Danny before murmuring something about grabbing a shower.

Stacy waved him off before stepping into the small maisonette and shut the door behind her. She locked and bolted the door and strode straight into the bathroom for a shower. The hot water soothed her as soon as she stepped in, temporarily numbing the constant feelings of panic that attacked her with each passing second. She wished that Danny could be there with her, to reassure her that everything would be ok. He was gone now, and she was all alone and petrified for his safety.

The world wasn't fair, that had been apparent for years. But she had endured the hurt and the trials of life and emerged with Danny at her side. She shuddered to think where or what she would be without him, and the thought scared her to death. After a few moments, Stacy shut the water off and wrapped a thick white towel around her body before heading into the bedroom to change into a set of loose fitting jeans and a cotton shirt. She threw one of Danny's hooded jumpers on and felt a slight flash of warmth as she caught the slight scent of his favoured deodorant. She smiled slightly and sat lightly on the end of the double bed as the fragrance hit her.

She fantasized about being in his arms once more. It was all she wanted. As she sat there, she wondered idly about where he was now. Was he coming back for her right now? Was he already back and going after Carter this very instant?

She suddenly felt hopeful as the thought of whether he was in the tower block or not reached her mind's eye and she started as though to race to the door and check the corridor. She stopped herself then and put her face in her hands, knowing how foolish she was being, but she just couldn't help herself as the longing intensified.

A swift knock at the door startled her from her thoughts, and she rushed into the hall, hardly daring to believe that Danny was just the other side of the locked door. Stacy unlocked the door and threw it open with shaking hands . . .

And froze as she looked into the eyes of the man who had stalked her dreams since the night he had murdered Steve in cold blood.

"Hello Stacy," Carter smiled.

He raised his weapon, a silenced Beretta 9mm as the scream built in Stacy's throat, and she couldn't find it in herself as her eyes locked onto the pistol that was aimed to her chest.

"Good girl," Carter nodded in approval. "We don't want to cause a scene, do we?"

"What do you want?" Stacy asked in a frightened voice.

Carter grabbed her arm, turning her roughly around and marched her into the lounge before shoving her onto the sofa.

She noticed that he wasn't alone, as a tall, middle aged man with brown hair that was greying at the temples wearing a grey suit and trench coat joined them a few seconds later. She didn't dare move, even when Carter lowered his weapon.

The fear kicked in then, shooting through her system and taking over every thought and every movement. She tried to calm herself as she looked at the two men in absolute disbelief. She wanted to run, to get as far away from the killer that stood before her but there was no escape. She was trapped.

"Come now, that's a bit of a silly question," Carter chuckled. "You know exactly what I want."

Stacy shook her head frantically. She wouldn't betray the man she loved, even if that meant death. That was something she'd gladly accept if it meant she could give Danny even so much as the slightest chance of survival. That would be some kind of victory, wouldn't it?

"He doesn't live here, if that's what you're thinking," Stacy squeaked.

She couldn't tell if the lie was convincing enough. She was too frightened.

"Your council doesn't protect the privacy of its tenants very well Stacy, I know full well that this is the flat you both share so please, don't treat me like an idiot."

"Why are you here then?"

"I want to know *where* Danny is, and I think you know the answer to that."

"Well you've had a wasted journey then," Stacy growled as she found just a hint of confidence within her. Danny was everything to her, and she couldn't and wouldn't fail him.

Carter shook his head in disappointment, and then brought the pistol to aim at Stacy's forehead. "Don't lie to me, as much as I'd hate to kill you, Harcourt here won't be so merciful."

"I would rather die . . ."

"Don't be irresponsible Stacy, what's more important to you, your country or your boyfriend?"

Stacy glared at him as the intense love and adoration she felt for Danny flooded through her. It numbed the fear and gave her the strength and defiance she had long since lost. It returned now with a vengeance, surging with a passion through every cell in her body.

"I know that he's somewhere in Scotland Stacy," Carter growled. "I promise you now; if you tell me where he is I will never bother you again. You can go right back to how your life was."

"If you expect me to let you kill my only reason for living," She snarled as she jumped to her feet angrily, "then you must really need that head of yours testing!"

Carter grabbed her arm, pulling her furiously towards him and pushed the muzzle of the weapon to her temple. She froze as she felt the cold steel touching her skin.

"If only he could see you now," Carter whispered in her ear. "Would he really expect this off you? Would he let you fight his battles and then die for him?"

"We protect the people we love around here," Stacy told him in an assertive voice.

Carter grew angry and threw her against the wall, pinning her against it as he flicked off the safety on the gun. "Last chance Stacy, now WHERE IS HE?"

Stacy glared defiantly into Carter's furious eyes. She was ready to die to keep the man she loved safe. And if Danny was alive, he *would* find Carter and he would kill him.

She flinched as he aimed the gun skywards and fired a single shot into the ceiling. Despite the silencer muffling the report it still sounded like a clap of thunder as the fear broke through once more, and suddenly she was afraid, afraid to die trapped and alone in her own home. She wanted Danny to burst through the door now and save her once more. She wanted it more than she wanted the oxygen to breath.

The gun came down to rest against her temple once more and she closed her eyes and told Danny that she loved him as she waited for death to claim her at last.

There was a soft clicking sound and for a moment she thought that it was over. Stacy opened her eyes as she felt the pressure ease against her pinned body to see Carter stepping back to holster his weapon. And she was relieved.

"Looks like we are doing this the hard way then," Carter murmured.

"And what is the hard way?" Stacy asked in a timid voice.

"If you won't lead us to him, we'll lead him to you. We'll be back at six pm tomorrow. Make sure Danny is here, or I *will* kill you," Carter advised her quietly.

He gestured for Harcourt to follow him and they stormed quietly out of the flat.

Once Stacy was sure they had gone she collapsed to her knees and began to hyperventilate again. Despite the momentary resurgence in defiance, the events of a moment ago had stunned her. Every time she closed her eyes she saw Carter aiming the gun at her and felt the pressure against her skin as he pushed the pistol against her skull. She needed Danny with her now as she slowly began to fall apart. He alone would be able to help her, and reassure her. She felt completely exposed and unprotected without him. And it was killing her.

*   *   *

Danny finished firing the fourth of the weapons that lay on the wooden floor just behind him and lowered the gun whilst he and Paul strode forwards to survey the devastation.

The cardboard targets were a broken, shredded mess and were full of ragged concentrations of bullet holes. Paul reached out with his hand as he approached and ran it slowly down the impact points as though he was indulging himself in a mid-air game of dot to dot. Danny looked carefully at the heavily compacted bullet concentrations; it appeared that he had inherited his father's shooting ability. Would he have been proud of him?

A small but assertive voice at the back of his mind told him in no uncertain terms, *no!*

Danny knew that his father wouldn't want him to use his destructive new talent in anyway shape or form, and that included pursuing his vendetta against Carter. But whether Danny decided to listen to reason or not was a different matter entirely. His new found ability unnerved him even now and he couldn't help but be a little scared.

"What's the verdict then?" he asked Paul quietly.

Paul didn't answer right away as he removed the broken pieces of cardboard from the room. When he returned a second later he looked carefully into Danny's eyes as he hesitated.

"I think that anybody who gets pulled into a firefight with you would have a serious death wish. Your shooting ability is *frightening.*"

Danny flinched slightly as Paul emphasised the last word, hardly daring to believe that after all he could have a chance of survival in a straight fight with the man who had plagued him the past week.

"So if he was to burst through that door right now, I could take him down?"

"You need to understand that the shooters that were drafted into The Rogues were the best of the best, and I reckon that hasn't changed. But yes, I think you might just take him with shooting like that," Paul replied assertively.

"It's good to hear that I've got a *chance* then. But like I said, I'm picking my girl up and then we'll go wherever the road takes us."

"He isn't going to stop looking for you Danny; he'll chase you to the end of the earth and back until he kills you. This is the one battle you have to fight if you want to live out your life with that girl of yours and believe me, he'll use her against you."

"Let him try," Danny growled angrily. "Thanks for the help Paul; I think I should get going before it gets dark."

He threw the weapon to the ground and stalked quietly out of the hut and into the rain.

"So that's it then, you're just going to give up?" he demanded loudly as he strode after him.

Danny froze halfway to the main log cabin. The rain drifted lazily around them as he turned to face him.

"Who said I'm giving up?"

"Well you tell me your plan then Danny because at the moment, you're walking both yourself and Stacy blindly to your deaths!"

"I DIDN'T WANT ANY OF THIS!" Danny snarled back at him. "All I've wanted my entire life is to be different from the others. I don't want to be a killer and I certainly don't want to be stuck in Leigh Park watching the telly and eating beans on toast for the rest of my life. Everywhere I turn there's yet another obstacle getting in my way!"

"What were you expecting, an easy ride through life? I'm sorry to tell you this Danny but LIFE ISN'T FAIR!"

"You think I don't know that?" Danny snapped.

"Well why don't you be a man and fight for the people you *claim* to love then?" Paul challenged furiously.

Something snapped deep within Danny, and he started towards Paul angrily. He stopped himself out of respect for his dad; he wouldn't want his son to beat his best friend to a pulp, even if he was provoking him. He stood there and glared murderously at the man before him before turning on his heel and storming off into the main cabin.

Paul followed him slowly and regretted his outburst. He knew that Danny wasn't to blame and he shouldn't have tried to provoke him, however he wasn't about to apologise for it. Danny was going about this all wrong and he didn't wish to read in the papers about his death in a couple of weeks' time. He shook his head angrily as he cursed aloud.

*   *   *

They strode quietly away from the tower block, not bothering to look back as they climbed into the waiting car. It pulled away immediately, winding its way through the deserted and sopping wet streets.

Carter glared out of the back window as the buildings whipped past. He was thinking of the best way to draw Danny into his clutches in such a short amount of time. And with the attack planned for a day and a half's time, he was already feeling the pressure.

"She doesn't know where he is Alistair," Harcourt told him in a restrained voice.

"I'm not convinced," Carter replied quietly

"Were you really expecting her to tell you?"

"Give it a rest Harcourt."

He complied reluctantly.

"We have two days until the main operation begins, so we have to find Patterson and we have to find him soon," Carter continued after a moment.

"Yes well why don't you let me worry about finding Patterson, in the mean time you need to finalise our plans and coordinate with the cell in Aldershot," Harcourt told him persistently.

Carter nodded, not bothering to argue with Harcourt as the car sped away from the town.

*   *   *

In the hour following their argument, Danny and Paul said nothing. The silence infected the atmosphere like a disease as they glared at each other. After what felt like a day, it had been Danny who had apologised first and was greeted by Pauls own apology. Paul then moved off to the kitchen to fix them up some food. He turned a radio on and turned to volume to a level where Danny could hear it. A catchy Coldplay song filled the log cabin, suddenly lightening the mood like a ray of sunlight breaking through the clouds. Danny even smiled as he recognised it.

He stepped through the room, passing the roaring log fire and emerged in the doorway to watch Paul as he fixed them both a bacon sandwich. The smell of the bacon cooking under the grill reached him after a brief moment and he was immediately reminded of home. In his mind he saw himself cooking romantic meals for himself and Stacy at night, knocking up sandwiches for the boys whenever they invaded his flat, and he wished he could have that old life back. He missed quiet nights on the sofa with Stacy in his arms and a film on the television. Even the beans on toast weren't bad . . . when it was Stacy's turn to cook. It was the life he had always dreamed of.

"Have you got a spare set of clothes and a rucksack?" he asked.

"Look in the bedroom and pick what you want, my stuff should fit you quite well. I'll find you a kit bag in a minute," Paul replied with a nod.

Danny smiled slightly and then strode back through to the living room, finding the bedroom with ease and began to rifle through the clothes in the drawers. After a few moments, he picked a set of dark jeans and a long sleeved shirt and quickly changed out of his soaked clothing. When he was done he looked around the log cabin, keen to explore it as he marvelled in its beauty.

He had always dreamed of having a place like this one day, just a little thing that would suit him and Stacy down to the ground. *She'll get a kick out of a place like this,* Danny told himself with a smile. *One day.*

Danny made his way back to the kitchen, where Paul was plating up a set of sandwiches for them both. He went to stand by the breakfast bar and Paul pushed his plate towards him a second later. Danny picked up the top sandwich and bit into it quickly. He hadn't realised how hungry he was until now as he wolfed down the salty bacon and buttered pieces of bread. He had to admit, it tasted good, much better than what he had ever managed in his lifetime.

"How the hell did you manage all of this?" he asked Paul with curiosity.

"I got lucky on the lottery back in 2000," he replied almost guiltily.

"Fair play," Danny chuckled. "Is there a tumble dryer here, or do you have a river out the back to wash your clothes with?

Paul choked on a bit of his sandwich, before turning to face him. He smiled slightly. "Of course I've *got* a bloody tumble dryer. Just because I'm from Chichester . . ."

"I get it, you've got one," Danny grinned. "That leather jacket I had on, I'm pretty fond of it, even if I did nick it from someone's house back in town. Any chance I could bung it in there to dry?"

"Leave it to me," Paul nodded.

Danny smiled again before turning back to his food. He liked Paul; he was easy to get on with, when he wasn't being a *grumpy ginger git.*

His thoughts turned back to Stacy as he wondered idly if she was okay, and as always, the worrying was persistent and at the forefront of his mind. He smiled to himself as he thought of holding her in his arms again, the feel of her soft skin on his own, the smell of her hair as he ran his hand through it delicately. It intoxicated him as he thought of her.

He heard the song that was currently on the radio end and then the DJ began to proclaim in an exited and slightly hyperactive voice that it was the greatest song around. Another song started up and Danny realised with a pang of grief that it was Steve's favourite song. He zoned out and became lost in the maze of grief that seemed wedged in his mind. When he snapped to attention about thirty seconds later, he realised that he had heard his name on the radio. He asked himself quickly if he was being paranoid, only for the little voice in the back of his head to answer *probably*.

He froze as he listened to the message that the hyperactive DJ was reading out:

> *I just want to get a quick shout out to my old friend Danny Patterson, who's been knocking around the Dunfermline area on his little business trip. Your dad is dead proud of you and Stacy wishes you would hurry home because she misses you like you won't believe . . .*

Danny's breath hitched in his throat as the shock took over. He recognised the threat in the message. It was thickly veiled, but present nonetheless. And it terrified him.

> *Can't wait to see you all tomorrow evening at six, Alistair . . .*

Paul froze as he recognised the threat as well, and swiftly whirled to face Danny who was visibly shaking with anger.

"Danny?"

"You were right," Danny whispered. His voice was layered with fear and it was laced with blind fury. "I need to go."

Paul threw out his arms to hold Danny back.

"No, that's what he wants! He wants you angry and scared because he knows that you'll come for her," he urged him quickly.

"I can't leave her in his clutches! I'll kill him, I *swear* to you now . . ."

"It won't be enough; He'll have everyone he's got looking for *you*!" Paul responded assertively. He held firm as Danny continued to attempt to barge past him.

"Well help me then, Stacy is everything to me and I can't lose her!" Danny pleaded quickly.

He stopped trying to get past him and looked frantically into his eyes. "Paul, please?"

"Yes, okay, but for god's sake listen to me first," Paul groaned as he moved his arms away from Danny, who in return stepped back himself.

"Carter is playing some sort of perverse game with you, I can see that now. The thing is *you* are the underdog. Carter knows his stuff, and you can bet he'll have a base of operations down towards Pompey.

"If you take out his backup you'll even the odds and then you'll be able to get to him. Do you understand?"

Danny nodded. It sounded easy enough. The anger and fear refused to subside as Paul continued to advise him.

Carter had crossed an invisible line and attacked the girl he loved, and as a result there was only one response for Danny to make. It was time for him to enter the game.

11. Combat

The air was full of a mad hum of differing musical styles as the carnival moved into its full swing. The drums beat steadily, reverberating across the town as the procession slowly snaked through the crowded streets of Leigh Park, and I wondered if they could sense the danger in the air whilst I sprinted through Park Parade and out into the road.

Carter raced for the fair ahead of me as the drumming pitched up a level and pounded a swift, hypnotic beat. As I threw myself into the road, I remembered the legend about the sound of the drums, and it was like I could hear their warning beats echoing through the streets as I chased my enemy down.

D anny stared impatiently out of the window as the train departed the platform almost lazily. It felt as though it had no idea of the rush he was in.

After a few moments, Danny shrugged away from the window and made his way carefully through the carriages, just thankful for something to take his mind off his worries. If he was honest, the radio message had unnerved him, and it had proved once-and-for-all just how determined Carter was to find him; *and kill him.*

Even after the half a days' worth of travelling, the words still rang in his ears as though they were being spoken aloud and Danny simply had to look behind him as he moved steadily towards the front of the train. The thick leather jacket he was wearing hid the weapon well; The Browning Hi-Power rested in the inside breast pocket and came with two clips worth of bullets . . . *insurance*, Paul had told him before he had helped him in his attempt to return south.

He had promised to join him as soon as he could, and to be honest Danny was happy that he had. He needed his advice and his guidance more than he had ever let on. He considered Paul a father of sorts, even if he would never admit it.

Danny gripped the back of the seats in front of him as the train began to slow down; he felt those powerful brakes being applied as the floor under him shifted slightly with the loss of momentum. He glanced outside and saw the suddenly reassuring sight of the houses that he knew only too well. He was home at last. Danny smiled slightly with the thought before slipping his free arm through the strap to pin the rucksack to his back. He loosened the straps slightly as the platform appeared outside. He wanted to be prepared for anything, and freedom of movement would be a huge advantage if he needed to react swiftly.

The train slowed to a halt this time and passengers started flooding out of the carriages towards the pneumatic doors at either end. Danny glanced behind him once again, and suddenly imagined himself as a soldier on a World War Two landing craft. A second later the doors hissed and slid open and Danny stepped quickly onto the platform. He glanced quickly up at the sky to see the light quickly fading.

That worried him. It removed all advantages he held in terms of actually knowing the area, and if he couldn't see who or what was around him . . .

Danny shuddered with that thought as he strode quickly through the ticket barriers and out onto the street. He moved quickly, sticking to the lit up spots as much as he could as the light hints of the day vanished with the advancing darkness. The moon rose in the east as Danny made his way quickly though quiet, deserted streets and he could almost sense the tense, flammable atmosphere looming around him ready to spontaneously combust at any moment. He could sense the threat in the air, and it just made the eerie feelings all the more potent.

He checked the time and realised that he was early as he jogged across the street to avoid an incoming car. He stuck to the lit up area now as he spotted the familiar opaque silhouette of the chemical tanks in the industrial estate half a mile ahead of him and turned into an alley, striding quickly through the darkness until he emerged into the light cast by the yellowish coloured streetlamps and stopped to look up at the tower block that he recognised so well. The structure was full of lights as the night took over what was left of the daytime.

He smiled slightly with the thought of home. He could see it now, on the fourth floor, facing west was the window of his living room and the lights were glowing brilliantly inside. He thought of Stacy, up there, scared and alone. And before he knew it he was striding forwards and broke into a jog. He glanced behind him to check that the streets were clear; he didn't want to be ambushed when he was so close to her. Crossing the road at a swift pace, he was engulfed by the darkness once more as he crossed the lawn and re-emerged a moment later at the security door. He fished the key out of his pocket and slipped in into the lock. It clicked as the locking bolt retracted and he threw the door open and half ran into the building. The tower block was a maze of prefabricated concrete corridors, stair cases and flats, something that unnerved Danny as he moved quietly towards the first staircase just off to the left hand side. Danny didn't trust the lifts that were just down the hall; they always had a reputation for breaking down between floors. He shuddered with the mere thought of it as he paused to retrieve the Browning from his jacket pocket. He flicked the safety off and raised the weapon, ready to fire as he began to climb the stairs.

It was slow progress as he took each flight slowly; taking great care to ensure that he was alone.

Soon enough he reached the fourth floor and sidestepped into the main corridor. He checked his back once again and moved through the corridor, dropping his aim slightly as he closed in on the flat where Carter was holding Stacy. He flattened his body against the wall as he reached the flat, and reached out with his right hand to run his hand softly down the frame of the door as he checked for booby traps. Paul had told him about those, and it sounded quite nasty. He didn't fancy being blown to hell and back by some Semtex and a tripwire.

When he was satisfied, Danny pushed the door slightly. It moved with his hand as it began to swing away from him. He withdrew his arm and brought it back to support his firing hand as he kicked away from the wall, bringing the weapon up and turned to cover the entry point. He moved silently into the flat, shutting the door behind him and advancing into the short corridor. The first thing he noticed was how quiet it was as he worked his way silently through to the living room.

Where was everyone?

Danny lowered his arm as he stood in the middle of the room, glancing around edgily. His mind was screaming danger at him and he wondered if this was a trap. He heard voices issuing quietly out of the kitchen just off to his left and slipped his rucksack quietly to the floor and raised the gun. He strode quickly towards the closed door, ignoring its white paint as his hand came down around the handle. He tightened his grip on the weapon and took a deep breath . . . and shoved the door open.

It slammed against the wall, making the two occupants jump as he sidestepped into the room, weapon up and ready to fire.

Danny froze as he looked into a pair of terrified hazel eyes and recognised the two people in front of him with a pang of guilt as the knowledge that he was about to open fire on them struck him. He looked into Stacy Ryan's rich hazel eyes again and he could have cried. Her still form, half clutching at the breakfast bar behind her shook with fear as she stared at the gun in his hands and he was sure that she had believed that he was actually Carter.

Danny locked the safety and tossed the weapon onto the side, before stepping swiftly across the room to wrap his arms around the girl he loved.

"I'm so sorry about that Stacy," he whispered as she pulled him closer.

She moulded her body to his and kissed him almost violently. He responded, allowing her insistent lips to mould to his, and in that moment he knew that he was home. It was as though of the worry, all of the heartache and all the concerns about his vendetta with Carter had disappeared as they lost themselves in their own world.

Danny pressed his hand to the small of his back as they kissed, pulling her closer and ran his hands through her silky hair. He was happy at last.

He finished what he had started after a few moments, pulling away to look into Stacy's eyes. He saw that they were alive with love and alive with relief; it was as though they were physically sparkling, like gems. Danny smiled slightly.

"I love you," he told her quietly.

Stacy merely smiled as she pulled him closer. She rested her head against his shoulder and closed her eyes, no doubt finding that security she always felt in her arms.

"Well this is all very dramatic and lovey dovey, but it's nearly six and he's going to be here at *any* minute," Bill told him in an assertive voice.

"Then you should get out of here whilst you still can," Danny replied quietly.

"I'm sorry Danny," Stacy murmured. "Carter tricked me, and he threatened me. I was so *scared.*"

"I know he did, and I'll make him pay for it. I'm so sorry for leaving you like that," Danny vowed as he pulled away from her.

He turned to Bill, frowning slightly. "Was there a weird radio broadcast down here?"

"No," Bill replied quietly.

Danny glanced at the clock on the wall behind him and groaned. The clock read six exactly, and that meant Bill was trapped with them.

He snatched up the gun that lay on the side and sprinted into the front room with Bill and Stacy hot on his heels and glared out of the window. Down in the darkness he could just make out three figures advancing quickly towards the flat and his throat tightened with the realisation that he was out manned and out gunned. He needed Paul, and he needed him now. He was out of time.

*   *   *

Carter led the way into the tower block, moving swiftly through the darkness with Harcourt and Newton on his flanks. He thought idly about what he was about to do. Was it fair to kill both Danny and the girl?

She was only looking out for her boyfriend after all; there was nothing wrong with that, and she was technically a civilian. But what if Danny *wasn't* there?

Carter had promised to kill her if he wasn't in there, and if push came to shove, he would kill her. That would be a guaranteed way to bring him back to where *he* wanted him.

He reached the door then and hit the *trade* button on the panel. He lock clicked open and he held it open as the others went inside. He followed, making his way back to the front and retaking the lead.

*   *   *

"Stacy, do you trust me?" Danny asked as he spun quickly to face her. He had an idea and he fervently hoped that it meant that she and Bill, at least, would be able to get out alive.

Stacy nodded quickly and Danny could see the fear re-appearing in her eyes . . . this time there was nothing he could say to comfort her. He turned to Bill, who smiled in anticipation.

"It's going to turn nasty?" he asked.

Danny nodded. "I'm going to draw them in here and whilst they're focussed on me, you're going to take Stacy and get as far away as possible . . ."

"No!" Stacy cut in quickly, "I'm *staying* with you Danny."

"Please don't make this any harder than what it already is; I don't want you to see this."

She crossed the room and grasped his hand, squeezing it tightly. She looked into his eyes and reaffirmed her refusal with as much authority as she could muster. "I'm staying."

Danny opened his mouth to argue, but quickly snapped his head up as the door rattled sharply. He pushed Stacy quickly against the wall, raising a finger to his lips. He backed off and slid quickly into the kitchen where he would be out of sight.

A few seconds later there was a crunching sound as the doorframe caved in. The door itself swung back on its hinges to crash into the wall. Carter, Harcourt and the third member of their party emerged into the front room after a second.

"I knew you'd tell him to stay away," Carter growled.

Danny raised his weapon then, emerging from the kitchen and swinging it like a club, he brought it crashing down on top of Carter's head. He buckled and collapsed as Danny lunged first at Harcourt on his left, landing a solid blow to the face that sent him sprawling to the floor and quickly spun to face the remaining member of Carter's hunting party, throwing himself at him as he tried to go for his weapon; he slammed him into the wall and then grabbed Carter as he struggled to his feet.

Danny directed his weapon at Carter's forehead as his companions swiftly scrambled back to their feet and aimed their own weapons at Danny and Carter.

"Hello Alistair," he said quietly as Carter groaned with pain. "Stacy, Bill move over to the front door."

They did as they were told, sidestepping around the confrontation as Danny nodded his approval.

"You didn't think this through, did you?"

"And what about you Danny, did you think this through?" Carter growled.

Danny laughed. "I don't care; my only aim is to kill you."

"The feeling *is* mutual."

"Was that what you told my dad when you bottled it in Iraq?" Danny growled, "You've killed two people who meant the world to me, now tell your goons to put down their guns so my friends can leave in peace."

Carter said nothing as Danny pushed the gun into his skull with more force.

He could do it; he could pull the trigger and end the life of the killer before him and have no regrets at all. It was the least the coward deserved after everything he had done. But could Danny really kill him in this way?

It wasn't honourable, or fair, but then again, when had that ever stopped the man who knelt before him?

Acting of their own accord Harcourt and Newton lowered their weapons slowly, and threw them to the ground in front of their feet

"Bill, take her and go. I'll find you later," Danny murmured after a moment.

"No!" Stacy screamed.

Danny glanced quickly towards her; she was struggling to fight back against Bill, who was pulling her out of the front door.

"Let me go, I'm staying!" she shrieked in desperation as Bill dragged her away.

Danny caught movement out of the corner of his eye and quickly snapped back to attention, pointing the gun at Harcourt who had tried to go for his weapon.

"Try that again," Danny snarled. "I dare you."

*   *   *

"Bill let me go!" Stacy insisted desperately as he steered her quickly towards the nearest set of stairs. "Let me go, he needs me!"

Bill ignored her, pushing her forwards and down the first flight of stairs. He didn't plan on hanging around; he trusted Danny and he knew he'd find them soon enough. He was just trying to give him and Stacy a chance to get clear before the carnage began. She kept struggling as he forced her down the next flight of stairs.

The quiet was almost eerie, with only the sound of their hurried footsteps for company. She tried to break free from his grip again and he stopped and grabbed both of her arms, rooting her to the spot as he turned her to face him.

"Listen to me Stacy; he's trying to give you a chance to get clear of danger. We *have* to use this window, and we *have* to believe in him. You two are going to need each other now, more than ever, you *must* understand that!"

"I don't care, he needs somebody with him!" she shrieked hysterically, her voice layered with distress.

"He'll be fine, he always is. Please . . . help him help us!" Bill promised her quickly. "I don't like the idea of running away at a time like this either, but we haven't got a choice."

Bill could see that she was trying to summon up what little courage she had left, and he fervently hoped that just this once she had decided to listen to him.

They froze as the first shot rang out above them.

*   *   *

"What are you hoping achieve here Danny?" Carter growled.

Danny laughed. Carter knew what this was all about. There was no point playing the fool.

"Ask yourself that question, you might surprise yourself."

"I'm asking *you*." Carter retorted angrily.

He remained still as he felt the cold metal finish of the pistol resting against the back of his head. He wasn't stupid, one false move and Danny would win. And this wasn't a game he could afford to lose.

"What are you planning?" Danny demanded.

"There's no planning to be done. This time tomorrow the country will have been put back on the path to greatness and changed for the better."

"What do you mean?" Danny pressed quickly.

He glanced at the two in front of him, both looking as though they were ready to throw themselves at him the second he let his guard down.

"This country is tearing itself apart because of a government that doesn't care. We will not allow it to happen anymore," Carter told him with a passionate voice.

Danny grimaced. So Carter was a *patriot,* great.

"What do I have to do with it? Why did you kill my best friend?"

"It was necessary!"

Danny raised the weapon above his head and let it fall back to smash into the back of Carter's skull. He cried out in pain as Danny let him fall. Harcourt and Newton went for their guns as Danny quickly sidestepped towards the corridor.

Newton was the quickest to snatch his up and raised the weapon as Danny moved towards cover. He fired, and the bullet whizzed past the spot where Danny had been just a microsecond earlier. Danny returned fire with a quick double salvo and Newton crumpled into a broken mess on the floor. Harcourt opened fire, and Danny turned on his heel to throw himself out of the room as a wall of lead slammed into the wall.

*   *   *

More gunshots issued from the upper floor, and Stacy broke free and began to frantically race up the stairs. She couldn't believe it, she wouldn't believe it. Danny couldn't be . . .

She couldn't bring herself to think that final word.

She shrieked as Bill pulled her back and began the struggle all over again and began to sob as she fought his grip, her worst fear seemingly confirmed. She jumped as another volley of shots rang out and only then did she become only vaguely aware of Bill desperately ordering her to come with him.

"Stacy . . . WE HAVE TO GO!"

She stopped struggling, and a second later the sound of rushed footsteps from the stairs above greeted them. They turned to sprint down the flights of stairs as the threat approached.

*   *   *

Harcourt raced over to help his boss to his feet, his face full of concern.

"Are you alright?"

Carter nodded as he clutched at his head. He could feel the warm, sticky substance on the back of his head and knew instantly that it was his blood.

"Get after him, we'll draw him to that fair down the road," he spat.

Harcourt nodded and led the way from the flat.

\

*   *   *

Danny raced down the corridor, throwing himself into the air and down the first flight of stairs as the sound of more gunfire filled the air behind him. He landed and slammed into the concrete wall before quickly shaking off the impact and sprinted down through the stairwell, taking the steps two at a time and he could hear movement both below him and above. He picked up the pace and could tell he was gaining on whoever was below him. He hoped that whoever it was they had enough sense to get out of the way.

He threw himself down the next flight of stairs as though he was a fun runner and caught up with Bill and Stacy within seconds. She threw herself at him, wrapping her arms around his neck as she stared at him with a mixture of shock, relief and fear. He ducked out of her reach agilely, snatching her hand and grasping it tightly.

"I think I've just stirred up a hornets nest . . . we need to go!"

Another gunshot from above confirmed that fact and she came willingly this time. They charged quickly down the last of the stairs and raced through the ground floor corridor. Danny relinquished his grip on Stacy's hand and spun on his heel, holding the line as he brought his weapon up in both hands.

"Get that door open!" he ordered.

"Danny, come on!" Stacy shrieked.

He glanced back at her. "Go now! I'm right behind you."

Harcourt spun round the corner and they opened fire on each other. The report from the firefight was deafening and the smell of gunpowder filled the air as they both dove for whatever cover they could find.

Bill grabbed Stacy as the two battled and powered through the closing front door and into the night.

Danny scrambled to his feet and withdrew quickly. He ejected the spent magazine as he ran and slipped the fresh clip from his pocket into the weapon before thumbing the hammer back to cock it. He caught the closing security door with his shoulder, barging his way through and raced into the street where Stacy and Bill waited for him to catch up. He skidded to a halt before them.

Let's split up, I'll take Stacy and head up to the Greywell; you find another route and alert Jack."

Stacy looked at him as he spoke and he could see that even though she was terrified, she looked determined to help.

There was movement in his peripheral vision and he turned to see two figures, the first he guessed to be Harcourt, who was heading towards them. The second was no doubt Carter, who looked to break off to the left hand side and cut through the housing estate.

Danny spun on his heel and grasped Stacy's hand as they raced through the streets and alleys that crisscrossed Leigh Park like the lines of a gigantic spider's web. Harcourt remained hot on their heels the whole time, never giving up as he pursued them without mercy.

They approached the Greywell after a few moments, and Danny glanced behind him as they slowed. Harcourt was nowhere to be seen as they strode quickly into the shopping centre and Danny couldn't help but wonder where the both him and Carter were. They strode quickly past the shops, and only the small Tesco express on the corner remained open in the otherwise deserted complex.

The loud booms of fireworks echoed across the sky, in tandem with a multitude of different colours as the fireworks exploded spectacularly. The distant sound of music and drums began to reach them as they pressed on urgently, only slightly muting the sound of the crowds that lined the distant streets to watch the carnival procession. Danny tried to find some comfort in the knowledge that it would be enough to prevent innocent bystanders from being caught in the crossfire. The silence was unnerving as he turned into a little bricked off seating area and turned to face Stacy. She looked scared, and rightly so, but he didn't want her to be caught in the crossfire either. He remembered the battle with Harcourt on the ground floor of the tower block and shuddered with the realisation of just how close she had come to being shot in that narrow corridor. No, this was a battle he had to fight alone.

"I want you to stay here and keep out of sight. I'm going to try and find Bill and lead Carter and his goon away from here," he told her quietly.

He looked into those hazel eyes to see them glistening not only with fright, but with adrenaline. He was sure that Stacy *felt* safe with him nearby, but when there was a large amount of hot lead flying about there was no such thing as safety. He could only hope that she understood that.

She nodded shakily, and her eyes began to positively blaze with fear. Danny felt as though his heart would break.

He pulled her into a swift embrace and pressed his lips softly to her forehead before releasing her. "I'll be back soon, I promise."

"Hurry," she whispered.

Danny gave her a slight smile, before turning away and strode away from her.

He searched the deserted shopping centre slowly and carefully, holding the gun down and slightly away from his body in both of his hands as he moved. The sound of more fireworks exploding filled the air around him as he moved around the complex and the lack of movement unnerved him as he searched for any sign of Bill. After scouring every inch, he turned and made his way back to where he had left Stacy to hide.

He heard the drumming sound grow louder as he strode back through the shopping centre and he could tell that the procession was getting closer. He thought about his old plans to take Stacy to see it and smiled slightly. He wished that all of this was just a dream. It wasn't what he wanted; he didn't want to be involved in some grotesque game of cat and mouse simply for the prize of *life* itself. It was all Carter's fault and there was simply no getting away from it. He was everywhere Danny turned, stalking him from the shadows and slowly turning him into the very thing he hated.

For some reason he stopped mid step, as though he could sense that something was not right. The eerie silence that fell between each boom and crash of the fireworks unnerved him. There was no movement in the darkness; the streetlights long since damaged and broken. It took him a slow second to realise that he was in fact back where he had left Stacy a few moments ago.

And she was missing.

Danny spun on the spot, looking in every direction in the hope that she would suddenly emerge from the shadows and throw her arms around his neck with an expression of relief. That nagging feeling of worry filled his mind and the thought of what could have happened terrified him beyond everything he had possibly imagined. He had failed to protect her in her moment of need.

He spun on his heel and strode back through the shopping centre once more, turning his head left and right as he searched frantically for her. He emerged into an open space surrounded by banks and more shops, all dark and locked up for the night. All the while he was vowing that he would find her *at all costs*. He turned right and stopped. He saw the mass of people lined up on the main road in the distance, lit up by the street lamps that hadn't yet been vandalised.

But what really got his attention was the lone figure that stood a good thirty yards away. Even in the darkness, Danny recognised the figure that stood before him, and he glared furiously into Carter's eyes.

"WHERE IS SHE?" he roared.

"I'm afraid that beautiful girl of yours has seen the light, Danny," Carter replied in a gleeful voice. "Play the game, and she may still survive in one piece. You wouldn't want *that* on your conscience would you?"

Danny charged then, his anger growing too great even for him to attempt to control. He chased Carter towards the street ahead of them, realising too late that the crowd of spectators lining that street were about to be caught in the crossfire. He decided that he didn't care; Stacy was in danger, and she was his only priority. Danny broke off as he saw Carter throw himself into the crowds ahead, turning to his left and racing through a small alley that ran between two shops. Danny emerged and sprinted towards the road, just in time to see Carter emerge from the crowd a moment later. He closed in as the carnival procession emerged from the main road and began to snake its way around the gyratory for the return pass. It was a solid mass of noise and light, consisting of a number of differing themed floats and people dancing or singing to the music. Leading them was a brass band, striking up a number of songs and marching to the beat of the drummers. They vaulted the crush barriers just a couple of seconds apart, and raced each other towards the procession. Carter got there first, slipping swiftly between two of the Lorries and racing off into the darkness.

Danny picked up the pace and rushed after him, getting clipped by the lorry to his left as he flung himself across the void. He gasped with pain as he hit the pavement awkwardly, but he scrambled to his feet anyway and threw himself back into the chase.

12. Love and War

They say that all is fair in love and war. And now as I prepared to fight my enemies for the sake of the very things I loved, I wondered if this was what they meant.

I remained outmanned, outgunned and outclassed as I fixed my furious gaze on the killer who stood before me, but I didn't care. This was about war and it was about love, of that I was certain.

This game was well underway, but there was no finish line in sight.

Danny moved through the funfair quietly and cautiously. Ever since he had seen the thriving mass of light he had slowed down to a walk out of caution in the darkness that enveloped part of the common. Something didn't feel right and he didn't trust the silence.

He moved slowly through the deserted fairground, turning his head left and right to check every angle and every shadow as he passed. His gun was in his hands and raised, ready to fire should he need to.

He knew he was here; playing his grotesque game of cat and mouse with him and using the girl Danny loved as the bait.

It was like some kind of unwritten natural law had been broken by his actions. Knowing that a girl was in danger was always more than enough to make a man change in his desperation to protect her and Danny was no different. He despised himself for what he had done these past few days; the shooting of Greene, the chase through Scotland that had nearly cost him his life and cost his pursuers theirs as a result. Even the shooting of that unnamed gunman who was lying dead in his flat was enough to tip him into the abyss that was already occupied by so many.

The remorse welled up inside him, bubbling away and threatening to burn him alive as he continued his search. His feelings for Stacy were the only things that were keeping the remorse from consuming him, and his desperation to find her was quickly becoming dominant in his mind. Even the mere thought of her staring down the barrel of Carter's gun scared him to death as he stopped. He turned a full circle in the middle of the open space that signalled the centre of the funfair. He caught movement on the edge of his vision, and spun to his right to face Carter as he emerged from the shadows. He smiled slightly as he acknowledged Danny's presence as he halted just five metres from him.

"You've fought well Danny, I'm impressed. Colin would be so *proud!*"

"I'm only just getting started," Danny retorted angrily.

"Yes well I'm afraid that this is where our little game ends. Bring her over Harcourt."

Carter's voice was calm and smooth as velvet as he spoke, even if the apathy was more than apparent.

Harcourt emerged from the shadows then, forcing Stacy ahead of him as he levelled the weapon that he held in his hand towards the back of her head. Danny diverted his aim to them as they stopped beside Carter. Danny looked into her eyes, and could see the exact same amount of fear etched onto her face that coursed furiously through his body. She looked back at him apologetically as she sobbed, and Danny felt something snap inside him. The desperation peaked as he shook with anger and fear. He didn't know what to do, and he couldn't see a way to save her. Carter had won.

"Now then, I'm going to ask you to make one last choice; throw down the weapon and I will let her live. The alternative needs no explanation," Carter told him.

"Let her go!" he demanded quickly, "Stacy has nothing to do with this!"

"That's where you're wrong. She is your rock, is she not?" Carter chuckled.

"Alistair, please. Me and you can go to the marshes and finish this alone if that's what you really want. We'll finish this game, just LET HER GO!" Danny snarled desperately.

Stacy struggled against Harcourt's grip as she sobbed and froze as he felt the weapon press harder against the back of her head.

Danny started towards them but stopped as Carter raised his weapon. Danny diverted his own weapon back to Carter as Harcourt smiled at him vindictively.

"There's no sport in that Danny. Remember that it was you who decided to play this game," Carter replied quietly as he moved across to take Harcourt's place. He pulled Stacy roughly towards him as Harcourt began to slowly move off to Danny's left.

"CARTER I AM BEGGING YOU, LEAVE HER ALONE . . . IT'S ME YOU WANT!"

"Throw down the weapon," Carter ordered.

"Let her go!"

Last chance Danny!" Carter growled. He forced Stacy down to her knees and she began to hyperventilate between each broken sob.

Danny kept switching his aim between Carter and Harcourt as he desperately tried to think of some way to save her. He knew of only one; and that was to sacrifice his life for her. He should never have dared to face him . . .

Danny shook his head, his face a mixture of different emotions as he slowly lowered the weapon.

"I'm sorry Stacy," he told her as he threw the gun to the grass at his feet. He stepped back from the weapon and Stacy shrieked in denial as she attempted to force herself frantically out from Carter's grasp.

He grabbed her hair and yanked her head back. She gasped as the pain shot through her system and she stopped struggling.

"Your boyfriend is being a noble man isn't he?" Carter muttered in Stacy's ear.

"That's because *he* is a man," She replied in a half formed sob.

"I've done what you've asked Alistair, now let her go," Danny told him quietly.

He kept his eyes locked firmly on the still forms of Stacy and Carter as Harcourt strode towards him. He saw him lower his weapon as he drew closer and he recognised the opportunity that had just been presented to him, hardly daring to believe that he *could* have just a slight chance of saving her after all.

"I don't think I will Danny. You see I'm taking quite a shine to her and I have to admit, she really is quite pretty," Carter replied in a gleeful voice.

"If you even so much as think about touching her I'll . . ."

"You'll do what?" Carter retorted.

Danny shifted his body ever so slightly as Harcourt reached down to pick up the discarded weapon and lunged, grabbing Harcourt around the neck and forcing him back to his feet. He brought his fist back and let it snap forwards with a powerful drive into Harcourt's face. He crashed to the ground as Danny snatched up the gun and brought it up before Carter could react.

He fired twice and the shots echoed into the night like a cracking whip, both rounds slammed into Carter's shoulder and he crumpled and released Stacy, who stared at Danny with wide eyes and a look of absolute horror.

"Get the hell out of here Stacy!" He shouted as he turned to face Harcourt. He scrambled quickly to his feet and threw himself at Danny. He knocked the gun from his hands as they grappled and forced Danny backwards, slamming him into the crush barrier for the ride behind them.

Danny lashed out with another punch that connected squarely into Harcourt's temple, but was unable to shake him off as his hands closed around his throat. Danny felt his air supply being choked off as they struggled and his vision began to dim. His struggles began to grow weaker as Harcourt slowly choked the life from him and he told Stacy that he loved her as his air dwindled and his sight blacked out.

There was a noise, like a whip cracking that issued across the clearing and Danny felt the pressure ease against his windpipe. He slid to the ground as his sight returned and air flowed back into his grateful lungs.

He saw the body lying just off to his right, face down in the grass as he sucked in the air in large greedy breaths and then barely a second later he felt the lightest of touches on his shoulder as Stacy appeared in his line of vision. She looked horrified by what had happened as she dropped the gun in her hands and sunk to her knees in front of him.

He recognised the look on her face. It was the look that he himself had worn just after he had killed for the first time.

That was when he realised that Stacy had shot Harcourt dead. She shook with fear and violent sobs rippled their way through her as he turned his head and locked his eyes onto her still form. He leaned his arm over and pulled her on top of him, holding her tightly to his battered and bruised body as he comforted her in a quiet voice. He stroked the back of her neck and pressed his lips to the top of her head as she sobbed.

Bill, Jack and Ade emerged from the darkness a moment later and rushed over to them.

"Where's Carter?" Bill asked as he spotted Harcourt's body a few yards from where Danny and Stacy were slumped against the crush barrier. Jack stalked off to the place Danny pointed to as he continued to console Stacy silently.

Ade crouched down beside them and smiled at him.

"You can't resist a good bruise up can you Danny?" he asked lightly.

"Believe it or not all I want is a quiet life," Danny grumbled quietly in reply.

Ade chuckled and clapped him on the shoulder. "It's good to see you mate."

Danny smiled slightly before returning his attention to Stacy.

"He isn't here!" Jack called after a moment. "And I see people coming from the carnival; it's a good idea to get out of here whilst we still can."

Danny cursed angrily. He had been so sure that he had finished him off, but obviously not.

The game was still in play.

He released Stacy from his body and helped her stand, never once letting go of her as they began to walk slowly into the darkness. Bill picked up the Browning and handed it to Danny before he and Ade took up a defensive position on his left and right flanks. Jack brought up the rear, ensuring that they weren't being followed as they made their way to safety.

*   *   *

Carter had never been shot before, so when the bullets ripped into his shoulder it was no surprise that it caused him nothing but absolute agony as the impact sent him crumbling to the ground like a demolished building. He lost his grip on the girl as his body spasmed and before he knew any better it felt as though he was on fire. He struggled slowly to his feet as the girl rushed towards Danny and Harcourt and he used the chance to stumble into the shadows as he clutched at his burning shoulder. It took another few minutes before the shot rang out into the night and he knew that it had just signalled the end for Harcourt. It didn't faze him as he concentrated on his own survival.

He was shocked that Danny Patterson was able to fire a gun with such stunning accuracy; much like his dad had been able to. But that wasn't his concern as he made it to the road and slipped into the shadow of an old oak tree to make the most important phone call of his life.

*   *   *

Danny continued to whisper words of encouragement to a devastated Stacy as they moved slowly through the dark hallway and into Jacks kitchen. He pulled a wooden chair out from under the breakfast bar and helped her onto it.

She squeezed his hand as he made to move towards the sink to clean himself up and he turned back to face her.

"Don't leave me," she whispered in a shaky voice.

Danny knelt down to place both of his hands over hers and placed them over her heart. He looked into her eyes to see them positively spinning with fright. He could see the emotions raging through her, slowly dragging her into a place he wouldn't dare think of. He knew the feeling well; she was going through that period of soul searching that came hand in hand with murder.

Of course Stacy hadn't intended to kill Harcourt; she had simply panicked as she tried to help Danny in his moment of need. He knew that she was a good person and she would be fine one day. And he would help her to recover.

"I'm not going anywhere," he promised in a quiet voice. "I'm going to make you a hot drink and clean myself up, ok?"

She gave him a quick jerky bob of the head.

He got back to his feet and leaned in to kiss her before letting go of her hands and crossed the room towards the white kettle in the corner. He caught the eyes of the other three as he flicked the switch and he felt reassured that they were still behind him. He turned to face them after a moment, but he didn't know what to say.

"What happened to you Danny?" Jack asked after a few minutes.

"Are you on about the fairground?" Danny grunted in reply.

Jack nodded quietly.

"Carter happened, Jack. He threatened to kill Stacy if I refused to come back from Scotland to fight him."

"And then?" Jack prompted.

Danny shook his head as the kettle boiled over. "I don't want to go into it Jack, for her sake."

They all glanced at Stacy, who was sat in the chair with her legs tucked up into her belly as she kept her terrified eyes locked onto Danny's every movement.

"She saved my life tonight," Danny informed them with a great deal of pride. "Without her it would be me lying dead on the common right now."

"It's about time!" Ade laughed.

Bill and Jack both shot a worried glance at him.

Danny shook his head as Ade gave them a confused look. As much as he liked Ade, he just didn't know when to shut up. He allowed Jack to do the tea, and a couple of moments later he slipped a steaming mug full of the hot tea carefully onto the breakfast bar behind Stacy. He stood beside her, holding her hand as he sipped at his own drink. He gave her hand an encouraging squeeze as he placed the cup on the side and returned his full attention to her.

"I need to go back to mine, that rucksack has some stuff in there that I can't leave hanging around," he murmured as Bill leaned on the side next to him.

"Don't worry about that," Bill replied. "I'll go up there with Jack in a bit. You need to stay with Stacy; she needs you."

Danny smiled grimly. "Thanks mate."

"I'll put you three up for the night," Jack grunted from the corner of the room. "And then we'll get your flat re-done for you. There's going to be hell to pay when this is all over."

Danny nodded his thanks before quietly gesturing for him to follow him into the hall.

Stacy stared at him with wide, frightened eyes, but she let him go as Jack followed him into the dark hallway and closed the door behind him.

"You don't seem too happy to see me," Danny challenged quietly.

"You promised me you wouldn't go looking for him Danny," Jack retorted in a subdued voice.

"I know I did, and look where it got me. Stacy and I were nearly killed twenty minutes ago and you're worried that I lied to you?"

"You're right Danny, I'm sorry. It's been a rough couple of day's man."

"Join the club," Danny growled. "Listen, that rucksack; for god's sake don't go in it, the stuff in there really isn't for the faint hearted."

Jack nodded. "There was a rumour flying about that an old barn not far from here became a real hive of activity on the day of Steve's death. Apparently it was really sudden."

"You suspect Carter?"

"Damn right I do."

"I'll have to go and check it out . . . there's no point telling me not to Jack, I've got to end it and I've got to end it now. We won't be as fortunate next time."

"Damn it Danny, if you die it'll kill her!" Jack growled as he thumbed his hand towards the kitchen.

"Have you got any better ideas?" Danny growled as he shoved Jack against the wall and pinned him there. "I *can't* protect Stacy from him and his goons. He's better than me and he's got the resources to keep this fight up for a very long time. Now you have *no* idea how close I came to seeing her be killed right in front of me, and I will not let that happen again!"

Jack kicked himself away from the wall, shoving Danny off of him and holding his hands out to show that he meant no harm.

"We all know just how much she means to you," he muttered calmly. "And you know that we'll never allow anyone to harm her."

Danny shook his head quickly in disagreement. "This is different Jack. None of us have faced something like this before and you know it. Just help me to finish the job, and we can go back to our lives!"

Jack seemed to hesitate, before finally holding his hands up in surrender. Danny knew that Jack wanted it over just as much as he did, and it was no surprise if right this second Jack was being bombarded by the memories of his own murky past. He suddenly felt envious of Bill and Ade, the only two of his friends who didn't have any axes hanging over their heads or any skeletons in the closet. He fervently hoped that they, at least would be able to live out their lives in peace.

Danny smiled slightly at Jack, before turning his back on him and striding back to the kitchen.

An hour later, Danny scooped Stacy up in his arms and carried her down the hallway into the front room where Jack had shoved two sofas together for them. He placed her carefully down onto one side of the sofa and pulled a couple of blankets over her body as she shivered. She looked up at him, and attempted a slight smile which faltered at the edges. Danny bent down to plant a kiss on her forehead before crossing the room to meet Bill and Jack in the hallway.

"Remember; don't look in the rucksack, get back as soon as you can because I need you to look after her while I'm gone," Danny whispered.

"Don't worry mate, we'll be back soon," Bill clapped him lightly on the shoulder as he followed Jack out into the night.

Danny shut the door behind them and slipped back into the living room. He climbed onto the opposite side of the sofa to Stacy and wrapped his arms around her shivering body, pulling her close to him.

She hadn't said a word for the past hour; such was the state of absolute horror at what she had done. Danny knew the feeling of course, and it had changed him . . .

She rolled slowly and wrapped herself firmly into his arms. He looked into her devastated eyes before she buried her head against his chest and was thankful that some of the fear had seemed to have dissipated at last, even if she was tearing herself apart over it.

He brought his hand up to stroke it gently through her hair; she had always loved the feeling, it soothed her and it calmed her when she felt scared or angry. He felt her shudder ever so slightly against his touch as she lifted her head to rest on his chest.

"It's like there's blood on my hands," she whimpered quietly.

"I know," Danny replied in a calming voice. "It'll pass; you're going to be fine."

"I killed him Danny!" she moaned. "I killed him!"

She began to hyperventilate in amongst the half formed sobs as she cried into Danny's jumper. He pulled her tighter against his body to comfort her.

"You had to Stace, if you hadn't I would be dead right now. You're not a killer; you're a life saver!" Danny replied.

He let her cry; she would be better off exhausting herself out and sleeping.

"I'm scared Danny, I'm scared that I'll never be myself again," she murmured after a moment.

"It's just the shock. You'll be fine," he promised her.

He knew the feeling and he knew it well as she shifted in his arms.

"What did it feel like?" she asked as she turned her head to look at him, "when you shot Greene."

"There aren't any words that can describe it. It tore me apart and I honestly believed that my life was forfeit."

"Was I right to shoot that man?"

"Yes you were. You had no other choice," Danny told her before leaning in to kiss her.

"Then why do I feel like I'm in the wrong?"

"It's because it goes against your very nature, a shock to your system. It was the same with me."

"That night, when I looked into your eyes it looked like you were scared, but not worried about what you had done," she murmured.

"I *was* scared Stace, and there are no words to describe what I felt. Once the adrenaline died off I felt it consume me and I'll probably never understand how I survived those moments.

"I'll never recover from something like that because I did what I did out of choice, but you? You didn't have that choice so it won't stay with you for the rest of your life. One day you'll forget it even happened."

"Do you promise? I can't stand the hurt anymore," Stacy whispered as she snuggled into a more comfortable position against his chest.

"I promise," Danny replied in a smoothly comforting voice as he placed his arms back around her body. "Now try to get some sleep, my dark haired angel."

Danny felt her smile as she buried her face against his chest and curled up into a loose foetal position against him and before long only her soft breathing filled the room. Danny doubted that she was asleep, just that she was trying to.

There had always been something deeply calming about watching her sleep. Danny would stay up late with her wrapped in his arms as she slept the night peacefully away. He would marvel at the way a couple of rebellious locks of her hair would suddenly fall across her face and come to rest on her forehead just above her eyes. She would stir a few moments later and brush the hair back behind her ear before snuggling closer to him. He longed for those days when they had nothing but their own happiness and so many different hopes for the future they would share together. Somewhere deep inside his mind, Danny still hoped that the future he so desperately dreamed of would one day become a reality.

He smiled to himself as he thought of it and then a few moments later it was like he could visibly see it; that vision of their future and their happiness playing out like a movie right in front of his eyes. Stacy stirred as the grin grew wider, propping herself up on his chest and looking at him with a slightly confused expression. Danny turned his head to look at her and beamed brightly at her, before pulling her close to kiss her again. She leaned into the kiss, and pushed herself closer to his body as she kissed him with a real urgency.

He pulled away after a moment, tightening his grip around her body as he leaned his forehead lightly against her own.

"See, I told you that you would be alright," he grinned.

He listened to the frantic beating of her heart, and he fell in love with the sound all over again.

Stacy shot him a bemused smile at first, before slowly beaming her warm smile at him. It knocked the stuffing out of him as it always had and he felt his heart stutter slightly before he leaned over to kiss her again.

13. Endgame

When I was a kid I used to ask myself, "What will I be in ten years' time?"

Out of all of those answers and all of those dreams for my future, I could never have believed that I would become this.

Yes, I was a killer, but not in cold blood. When this first began I kept telling myself that I had a choice; the choice between what is right and what is easy, but now I knew conclusively: there was no choice.

I had to see this game to its conclusion and for me to survive it would take every last piece of my determination and my adoration for the girl I loved. As I prepared to face Alistair Carter for the last time, I dared to dream of peace and a future with my girl.

But I had no idea of the losses I would one day suffer, and it still kills me to this day.

D anny moved quickly, keeping ahead of the patrols that encircled the perimeter around the old barn. Now that he knew just who The Rogues were, what they were, he was finally able to fight back at last.

His plan was to remove Carter's overwhelming advantage in terms of numbers and firepower-with it; he still held the high ground.

It had only been in the last few hours that Danny and Carter had mounted any memorable form of assault on each other, as their cat and mouse game took on a risk like state of strategy and skill. Carter had struck first, with Danny gaining the upper hand before Harcourt captured Stacy. In those fleeting moments of desperation that followed, both he and Stacy had nearly perished as a result. Danny never wanted to see her in that position again.

Harcourt was dead and Carter was wounded, but Danny was no fool. He hadn't won and as long as Carter remained alive he remained a threat.

Now it's my turn to strike Danny reminded himself.

In his rucksack were four blocks of C-4 plastic explosive with a trigger mechanism that was connected remotely to a master detonator that sat in Danny's pocket.

He dropped into the undergrowth as another patrol almost ran into him. For a moment Danny was sure that he had been spotted, and he held his breath as the two guards stopped just a mere metre away. Time seemed to stop as they stood there; forcing Danny to silently withdraw his Browning Hi-Power after a couple of moments. He didn't want to kill them, especially not in cold blood and without provocation. But if that was what had to be done, then so be it.

Paul had, of course, had taught him the principles of killing, and it was without a doubt the hardest thing humanly possible. It was so much more than just steadying your aim and pulling the trigger; it was a death sentence for the poor bugger in your sights. In that moment you became the judge, the jury and the executioner. After the kill had been made, that was when the remorse really kicked in. Right away you began to question your actions; had you done the right thing? Had it been your right?

After that period of soul searching the reality of what you had done finally began to melt away and it left you a completely different person. Danny remembered the pain he had suffered after making his first kill just days ago; he remembered seeing the life drain from the cold blue eyes of David Greene before his body collapsed into a broken wreck at his feet. The remorse that washed through him in the hours that followed had almost killed him. Or it had felt that way at least . . .

Danny breathed a sigh of relief as the two guards began to move away and got back to his feet carefully. Deciding not to take any further risks he flicked the safety off and moved into the well-practiced weaver stance, pressing his right hand into his firing hand to give himself extra support and keeping the weapon pointed at the dirt as he made his way closer to the barn.

*   *   *

Stacy stirred from her sleep after an hour, slowly rolling onto her side and reaching out to pull Danny's arm around her. She found only thin air as her arm dropped lamely to the smooth surface of the sofa. It confused her as she ran her hand frantically across the cushions, still finding nothing. It scared her as her eyes snapped open and she sat bolt upright, squinting into the dark in the hope that he would appear from the shadows.

She scrambled off the sofa and strode quickly into the hallway to snatch up her trainers. She ignored the hushed voices that issued quietly from the kitchen as she slipped towards the front door and opened it to step out into the night. She glanced quickly up and down the street before half running along the path as she searched desperately for him. A few minutes later she heard her name being called from behind her, and she turned slowly to see Ade striding quickly towards her in a thick black jacket he wore to protect himself from the cold. He looked her up and down, noticing her red cheeks from the exertion and the expression of panic that layered every ounce of her facial features.

"It's not the best time to be out here alone Stace," he told her quietly as he scanned the street with his eyes.

"He's gone," she replied in a shaky voice.

"You know what he's like," Ade told her impatiently. "Carter crossed a real line earlier so he's hardly going to let that go, is he?"

Stacy shook her head disbelievingly, unable to shake the feeling that he wasn't coming back this time.

"Come on, let's get back in the warm," Ade urged as he raised his hand for her to take. He gave her an encouraging smile as she hesitated, before she gave in and followed him quietly back towards the house.

*   *   *

It was an old thing, falling apart at the foundations, Danny thought to himself as he approached the barn in a cautious manner. Part of the straw ceiling was missing, and the left side was completely exposed to the elements. He moved closer, and he could hear the first signs of activity that gave away Carter's position.

Danny melted into the shadows as the next pair of patrolling guards appeared. He began to plant the first of the explosives on the ancient brick wall as they moved on, and he then moved carefully around, sticking to the shadows as he placed the explosives one by one. He wondered idly just how spectacular this boom would be; enough to wake the neighbours and leave a dirty great crater in the middle of the desolated old field? Or just a damp squib that would blast The Rogues into the deepest pits of hell where they belonged.

Danny seriously doubted it would be the latter as he finished placing the last explosive near to what looked rather suspiciously like a set of petrol drums. He glanced behind him once more, and noticed a set of vehicle headlights; no doubt Carter and friends, heading up the drive towards his position.

Danny turned and quickly threw the envelope containing his message to Carter into the light where it could easily be seen and sprinted for the cover of the long grass, ducking down out of sight as the headlights from the car bathed his position in light as it passed him. He fished the detonator from his pocket and stood. He wanted Carter to see him; to know that it was him who had dealt the Ace card in their game. Saying that, Danny took no joy from what he was about to do, even if he would not mourn for their deaths. He flicked the arming switch as Carter drew ever closer, and then thumbed the button.

For just a second, time seemed to stop, but in that instance the entire area was illuminated in reddish light. As soon as time restarted, the pure noise of the explosion echoed for miles and the barn blew itself apart, erupting into a mighty ball of fire that rose spectacularly into the air. The shockwave came next, and anybody within a hundred yards of the fireball were either blasted off their feet or incinerated in an instant. It hit Danny like a steam train as he walked calmly away from the blaze, rippling across his jacket and almost knocking him off of his feet. He remained standing through sheer fortune.

For just one microsecond, Danny felt satisfied; as though the deaths of Carter's comrades had atoned for their commander's sins. He ignored the calls for help, recognising Carter's voice amongst them as he kept walking.

*   *   *

Carter surveyed the devastation with a look of absolute horror. He felt the extraordinary heat that the inferno was throwing off lapping on his face time and time again. The harsh smell of burnt flesh was already beginning to pollute the air as he began to clamber over the wreckage in a hopeless attempt to help his men. In all the years he had served in the armed forces and beyond, he had never seen destruction like *this*.

The old barn was just burning rubble now, and anyone trapped within would certainly be dead. As Carter fell helplessly to his knees he felt the anger burning red hot inside his veins. It was a vicious emotion that he hadn't felt in over a decade. He found the envelope on the ground before him, singed slightly by the flames and he reached down to scoop it up. He ripped it open and pulled the note out to read:

Portsmouth Harbour station; tomorrow at 9am, come alone.

He felt nothing but apathy for Danny now; no grudging respect remained for the man who was playing the game a little too well for his liking as he cast the paper furiously aside.

It was time to end it, once and for all.

*   *   *

Stacy, Bill and Ade looked up as Jack shot into the kitchen like a bullet. He skidded to a halt as a huge grin spread across his face, giving him the sudden appearance of a Cheshire cat.

"Just heard from Danny," he told them breathlessly. "It worked, Carter's base went up like a firework, and Danny now has the advantage."

"Good news," Bill muttered.

"Where is he?" Stacy asked in a weak voice.

"He's in Stubbington; he wants to make sure he's not being followed before coming home," Jack replied with a smile.

*   *   *

Danny rose with the sun, instantly snapping to alert as though there was danger and after a moment he groaned slightly and sat up. He pulled the Browning that Paul had given him from under his pillow and quickly inspected it. He made sure the safety was on and placed it quietly onto the table before clambering off of the sofa and kissing Stacy softly on the forehead as she slept peacefully away.

After getting himself dressed, he pulled the duvet up over her a little more and picked up the gun before striding into the kitchen. There he found the others sat quietly around the table with their drinks and breakfast, and they glanced round to see him as he moved closer, all the while shoving the gun in his hand into his inside jacket pocket. Danny shot them a quick smile as he turned away to do himself some bread and butter.

He wondered idly to himself if today was the day that his own luck would finally run out, god knows he had come close several times. Then there was the most important of questions; was he scared?

There was no doubt as to that answer. Even now, he felt the fear pulsing through his body without any form of mercy. It was natural to be scared, and of course Danny had long since accepted the fact of his own mortality. If it was his turn to die, then he would make damn sure that he'd at least take Carter with him.

Then again, he simply couldn't bear to leave Stacy alone. If he died, it would destroy her. And that was something he would never allow. She was his sole reason for living, and a world without her in was no world at all. He resolved himself then, and that little voice inside his head made a single vow with such force that it was like he was shouting it aloud, and he vowed to ask her if he survived his meeting with Alistair Carter.

He wolfed down the bread and butter sandwich like a man possessed and turned to look at his best friends. He felt nothing but pride as he took in their various dishevelled appearances and was honoured to have known them throughout his life. He knew that he was subconsciously saying his goodbyes, just in case he didn't come back . . .

The thought scared him to death and he began to shake as he suddenly clutched at the sides of the breakfast bar for support. His friends rushed to his aid then, and as much as he didn't want or need it, he was still thankful.

"It's today isn't it? You and Carter are going to finish it off," Bill murmured after a moment.

Danny nodded slightly. He couldn't speak as he tried to compose himself.

"You don't have to do this alone Danny, if you need the help . . ."

"No, it has to be the two of us," Danny murmured after a second. "I don't want you guys to get caught up in this anymore. Just promise me something."

"Anything," Bill smiled, "you name it, and we'll do it."

"If I don't make it back, promise me that you'll look after Stacy for me."

"You already know that we will mate, we stand together, remember?" Ade grinned as he clapped Danny lightly on the shoulder.

Danny nodded his agreement and smiled only slightly. "I'd better go."

"Not yet, you should say goodbye to her first," Jack told him quietly.

"Yeah, you're right," Danny agreed.

He composed himself as he strode determinedly into the front room. The others hung back as though to give them some privacy.

He sat on the arm of the sofa and stroked his hand through her hair as she slept. He watched her resting peacefully away and wished that they had had more time together. It just further reinforced the vow he had made just moments ago.

She stirred after a few moments, stretching lithely and turning her face to see Danny's own.

"Hey," he whispered. He struggled to smile for her, but it faltered and died within seconds.

Stacy sat up as she recognised the anguish that was layered into every feature of his face. Even his eyes seemed darker. It confused her. He was ok, wasn't he?

"What's wrong?" she breathed after a second.

"I have to finish what I started," Danny said. "It's just me and him now."

"You don't believe that you're coming back?"

Danny shook his head as his face fell.

"I have to consider that possibility . . ." his voice trailed off into silence.

"Don't go," Stacy pleaded. "Please?"

"I don't have any choice. But if I don't . . ." he couldn't say those final words. It hurt too much. "Just promise me that you'll look after yourself, for me?"

Stacy began to cry silently as she reached out to him, and he gladly took her into his arms and pulled her into the tightest of hugs. He shed a few tears as the reality of what he was about to do hit him.

"I love you," he whispered.

"I love you too," she replied in a hoarse voice. She leaned in to kiss him, and she tried so very desperately to keep him pinned against her body as he released her and pulled away after a few seconds. She watched him cross the room and open the front door.

"Danny?" she called quickly.

"Yes?"

"Come back to me . . ."

He smiled slightly, before taking that last step out into the open, closing the door behind him and taking in the sights of his hometown for what he believed to be the last time.

The endgame was upon him at last.

*   *   *

Danny had a lot to thank Paul for if he was honest, in the short twenty four hour stint he had spent with him Paul had busted a gut training him and helping him prepare for the battle with Carter and The Rogues. Without a doubt the lack of sleep and constant rigour of the training had rubbed off on him. Danny didn't hope to be the best, just merely able to defend himself whenever the enemy would next come calling.

His thoughts sprung back to Steve, as always he wondered just what he would have thought if he could see him now; the alertness, the familiarity with small arms and the game Danny and Carter were playing together. The two of them were locked in a grotesque and deadly dance. One wrong move and that was it. *Game over.*

The sun shone bright and warm overhead as the train glided to a halt at the platform and Danny stepped off the train and into the sun. A wall of heat hit him like a bullet to the chest and found the dark leather jacket he was wearing uncomfortable in the heat but he ignored it as he blended effortlessly into the crowd that swarmed towards the exit. When he finally broke free a few moments later he crossed the old access road and strode swiftly towards the covered seating area on the seafront that overlooked the Victorian warship on the opposite side of the harbour.

Portsmouth had a long, dark and difficult history. Originally a roman port, it had slowly grown with the years and during that time it had found itself under attack from the French on multiple occasions. Despite those difficult times its people had pulled together and had survived whatever had been thrown at it. Once upon a time it had been home to the vast majority of the naval fleets of the country and some famous faces and names. It had found itself, perhaps unsurprisingly under attack from the Luftwaffe during the blitz and had still pulled through.

A single man leaned against the railings on the waterside, his shoulders hunched forwards in what *looked* to Danny like grief and if it wasn't for the dark suit Danny would have merely dismissed the lonely figure before him as an innocent bystander.

He approached slowly, keeping his eyes fixed firmly on Alistair Carter's still form as he moved his hand towards the gun that rested in his inside left jacket pocket.

"So, Alistair, how did it feel?" Danny asked quietly as he stopped a metre from him. "Did you feel what I felt? Did you feel the *grief* and the *anger*?

"Did it tear you up as you watched your men die?"

Carter spun to face him and his hand twitched instinctively for his own gun. Danny's mouth twitched before spreading into a grin as he noticed the stubble that now covered Carter's usually immaculate face. His expression was one of absolute fury, a furnace of emotion that raged wildly out of control.

"You killed twenty men, Patterson. Was a single man's really life worth another twenty?" Carter spat furiously.

"You should have thought about that before you took my friends life away."

Carter glared at Danny, too furious for words.

"I told you I would come for you," Danny reminded him quietly.

"So, this is where it ends then, yes?

"Well that's a gold star for the murderer," Danny nodded with a slight smirk.

"I'm a soldier, *not* a murderer," Carter growled as he shrugged past Danny and headed towards the main road.

"Don't give me that, it may help you sleep at night, but the fact of the matter is simple; *you are a murderer,*" Danny emphasised the last words as he fell into step alongside him.

"And that makes you the fairy godmother I suppose?" Carter challenged angrily as they passed under an old viaduct and into the shopping centre. Danny ignored the jibe.

"This is very theatrical, Alistair, why am I not surprised?"

He wanted Carter angry; an angry man made mistakes, and one mistake was all that separated the margin between life and death.

And it worked. Carter cursed under his breath as his temper began to fail him. Danny glanced up to look at the Spinnaker Tower towering over Gunwharf Quays, dominating the skyline with spectacular ease as they worked their way through the throng of early morning shoppers. Shops flanked them on both sides with the road that led to the multi-storey car park right behind them. A train rolled past them up on the viaduct they had passed underneath just moments ago, temporarily deafening out the noise from the shoppers that surrounded them.

"So tell me, The Rogues plan to launch their attack in, what? Four hours?"

Carter stopped and glared furiously at Danny.

"Come on, Carter. You owe me that much at least."

"Do I?" Carter replied sceptically, raising an eyebrow as he glanced down to check the time on his wristwatch. Danny didn't miss it and at that moment, an odd sense of de-ja-vu hit him. It was like Carter was expecting something . . . or *someone.*

"Are we waiting for somebody? It wouldn't surprise me in the slightest if you were chicken enough to call in reinforcements," Danny told him with a smirk.

"Being *chicken* isn't a luxury I have, Patterson, and neither is *time.*"

"I'm sure you say that to your boss all the time, I reckon he'd be really proud of his star man with an attitude like that."

"You seem to be incredibly sure of yourself, don't you Danny?" Carter retorted irritably.

Danny stepped forwards, and despite Carter's superior height, he wasn't afraid.

"I don't need to be sure of myself Alistair; I'm the one who picked the short straw in all of this. Now I would have happily fought you alone, man to man the honourable way . . . but when you threatened the person closest to me *that* was when it grew personal."

"Well if you had keep out of my business like I told you to, we wouldn't be in this situation!" Carter growled again.

His hand jerked towards his gun and Danny imitated the action.

"Come on Carter, a crowd has never bothered you before. You could have had me as soon as I got off the train, but no. Instead we're stood in a public area because you want to be all dramatic."

Danny kept his hand gripped firmly on his weapon as he backed off slightly. He didn't trust the expectant look that was sat rigidly into Carter's features.

And he could sense that any moment now, the battle would begin. Danny wanted more of an advantage than having an angry gunman stalking his every move. And Carter *was* lethal in armed combat . . .

All he had was the crowds, and he just hoped it would be enough. He turned his body slightly, so that he could manoeuvre easier when the time came. And that was when he spotted a lone BMW 5 series on the road to his right. It sped down the road towards them, catching Danny's attention immediately. As he looked into the vehicle, he spotted four individuals who looked like the guards he had seen in Carter's car the previous evening. He was certain it was them as the car drew swiftly closer to them, and he spotted the grey semi-automatic assault rifle in the hands of the mercenary in the front passenger seat.

Danny went for the Browning at that moment. He brought the weapon up just as Carter performed the same manoeuvre. Danny knew he couldn't win when he was outmanned and outgunned. He twisted his body, bringing his weapon around to aim at the speeding vehicle and fired twice. Both bullets slammed into the driver side front wheel and the driver lost control as it slid off of the road at high speed, towards Carter, who managed to throw himself out of the cars path before it slammed bonnet first into the brick wall of the viaduct.

In the ensuing chaos, Danny turned and sprinted into the crowds of horrified shoppers, pushing and shoving against those in his way. The first sign that Carter was giving chase became apparent with seconds as the first crack of gunfire issued out behind him. A single bullet slammed into the floor behind him just as he diverted his course. He sprinted up the first set of steps he saw and a moment later more gunfire crackled in the air around him as he threw himself up the last few stairs and onto the balcony, scrambling behind the wall on the concourse as a hailstorm of bullets smashed into the masonry. He poked his head out into the open to spot Carter and the four passengers from the ruined car sprinting through the panicking shoppers after him. Danny opened fire blindly, not bothering to check if he had hit anyone.

He heard the first metallic clangs of footsteps on the stairs as they advanced towards him and he turned his back once more and dashed flat out across the concourse in the hope that he could find a way out. More gunfire crackled from below and the shop windows around him shattered as the bullets hit them. He reached the end of the concourse then and looked around wildly for some sort of escape. It was a dead end.

Two of the gunmen emerged then, and Danny brought his gun up ready to fire. They hesitated, and that was all Danny needed as Carter advanced from below.

He fired once and the Browning kicked back angrily as though it had a point to prove. The gunman in the lead collapsed back into his partner, sending both of them sprawling to the ground as Danny vaulted the railings and dropped the ten foot to the ground. He landed awkwardly as another round whizzed past his ear and he rolled as his ankles protested against the force of the impact. Ignoring the pain, he spun himself onto his back and opened fire on Carter and his assault rifle wielding buddy, forcing the both of them to seek cover as the remaining man from the concourse appeared at the railings. Danny scrambled back to his feet, keeping the weapon up and took the man above out with a volley of shots then raced through the now deserted square.

Carter and the last of the gunmen tore after him. They emerged into the streets after a moment, and Danny turned on his heel, brought the weapon up and fired again. Carter threw himself out of the line of fire as his buddy stumbled and crumpled into a broken heap before him. Carter returned fire as he advanced quickly towards Danny, who had already turned and began racing swiftly through the crowds that populated the road. A few minutes later, Danny tore around the side of the ferry port and sprinted through it as more gunfire crackled around him.

He could feel his body growing tired from the exertion and so he began looking around wildly for somewhere to finally make his stand. He spotted the old stone tower at the front of the harbour and pushed on regardless of the lack of oxygen. His body protested furiously as he raced through the old cobbled street, pushing past horrified bystanders and dodging incoming cars whose occupants bellowed angrily in his direction as they swerved to avoid him.

He saw the old tower looming ahead of him and as he glanced back he saw Carter halt and raise his weapon; saw him aim carefully towards his back. Danny threw himself into the air as Carter opened fire and he felt the bullets whizz past him, dangerously close to where he been just a millisecond earlier. He crashed awkwardly to the ground and lost his grip on the Browning; it spun wildly away from him and came to rest underneath a car that was parked up just ahead of him. Danny scrambled to his feet and threw himself behind the cover of the dark blue Fiesta as Carter opened fire for a second time. Danny ducked down as he came under fire, lunging desperately for the gun that continued to elude him. He felt exposed and defenceless for the first time. He could see Carter moving swiftly in his direction, and if he reached him now, it would be over.

He lunged again and this time he succeeded. He dragged the gun into his hands and scrambled to his knees before firing blindly over the top of the car. Carter took cover and that was when Danny surged to his feet, vaulting the bonnet of the old Fiesta and sprinted down the final stretch of road before launching himself though the old door that led the way into the tower.

The acrid smell of seawater and seaweed struck him as he powered up the spiral staircase. He charged into the open space on top of the tower, decorated with a couple of showy old Cannons to find it empty.

That's good, Danny told himself as he stopped and turned to meet Carter's advance. This was where he had to draw the line.

Around half a second later the man himself emerged from the stairs and skidded to a halt as Danny moved to intercept him with his weapon aimed high.

"That's another four men you've killed Danny; now tell me we aren't the same!" Carter roared.

"We're nothing alike, Alistair. It was me or them!" Danny retorted angrily. "And now it's just the two of us."

"You don't have a point to prove Danny, and believe me I know. Just what are you hoping to achieve?"

"I want the life you stripped away from me back. I promised you that you *would* pay for the damage you've done. Now look at us! *You* turned me into what I am now. WAS THAT WHAT YOU WANTED?"

Carter glared furiously at Danny as they began to circle slowly.

"Later today, that life will all be gone, not just for you but for everyone in this country."

"I know about your plot to take over this country. And so do the authorities, you'll never succeed."

"They know about the *rumours* Danny, nothing more. I would have thought that you would have realised that rumours aren't always rooted in truth! After all that's what your street legends are all about."

"You don't know that!" Danny growled.

"We've been planning this for over a decade; do you *really* think we would let the truth be known now?"

Danny grimaced as he recognised the truth of the matter, of course, if they had been planning a revolution then they would have kept it top secret out of necessity. He only hoped that Paul would be able to get to him before it began.

"The army won't let you . . ."

"HALF OF THIS COUNTRY'S ARMED FORCE IS UNDER OUR CONTROL!" Carter screamed back at him. "We will topple Britain Danny, because we have to. This country is sick, and we are the only ones brave enough and capable of healing her.

"The national debt, immigration, rumours of Scottish independence. The government is too busy throwing us into wars that we can't afford to fight, and then they give our troops the middle finger when they leave the services. It is us who can stop the things that plague this country day after day."

"Don't give me that, you'll turn the country in on itself."

"It's for the good of the nation Danny. If the Government won't act to stop the British people from destruction, then *we* will!"

Danny lowered his weapon as they stopped circling. He locked the safety and tossed the gun to the side. He raised his arms slightly to indicate that he was now unarmed. Carter held his ground.

"You're going to have to topple *me* first Carter. Let's do this the proper way shall we?"

Carter locked the safety on his Beretta and imitated Danny, throwing the gun away from him before stepping forwards to meet him.

Danny smiled. "I guess you're not a coward after all, just a cold hearted bastard."

Carter lunged at him then, and Danny dodged nimbly before landing a solid blow to the side of Carter's jaw. He rocked backwards with the impact as Danny laughed.

"Come on Alistair, I'm sure you can do better than that," he taunted quietly. He moved on the balls of his feet as they circled once more.

Carter threw himself forwards and slammed into Danny. They collapsed to the stone floor and struggled furiously. Danny threw Carter off him and landed a quick succession of blows clean into Carter's gut before scrambling back to his feet.

Carter recovered and charged again. His fist connected with Danny's body, who stumbled back with the force of the impact. He had no chance to defend himself as Carter landed blow after blow to the face and chest, putting all of his strength and all of the hatred for Danny into each and every strike.

Danny felt the warm feel of his blood on his face as his body took a pounding. He imagined Stacy, all alone and desperate for news over his safety. He couldn't bear the thought as Carter's arm snapped back to finish him off and he reacted quickly, bringing his arm up to parry the blow and sprung the counter with a powerful strike back directly into Carter's stomach. He staggered back with the blow and Danny threw himself back into the fight. He grabbed Carter and pounded blow after blow after blow into whatever part of his body he could reach. He kept going, avenging the name of everyone who had perished as a result of his actions. With every hit he felt as though their memories would finally be put to rest, and Alistair Carter would never be able to destroy anybody else's life . . .

Out of nowhere, Carter finally fought back, and he sprung back to his feet, knocking the both of them over the side of the staircase. Danny turned his body at the last possible moment and it was Carter who took the brunt of the impact.

Danny felt as though he had just had an anvil dropped on top of him. His body felt as though it was screaming with pain due to the impact and he struggled feebly to his feet before stumbling back up the stairs. He managed to reach his gun but collapsed against the wall, the pain becoming too much. He tried to control the pain, breathing in and out deeply, using the oxygen as pain relief. The gun nestled in his hand, and he checked the magazine quickly.

He had a single bullet left and he fervently hoped that would be enough as he struggled to his feet. He felt the blood drying across the left side of his face and grimaced as the wound throbbed furiously. He swayed slightly when Carter appeared, his clothes torn and face bloody and broken. He raised the gun as Carter threw himself towards his own. In just a second Carter had snatched his gun and spun round, his finger tightening on the trigger.

Danny's aim dropped and his sight blacked out. He didn't even hear the weapon make a noise. He was dead, and he had failed. Danny said his goodbyes to Stacy as the blackness dissipated. His sight returned now, and a strange clicking noise issued from Carter's weapon. Danny understood immediately as he focused his gaze on the bloodied man in front of him. And he was thankful that he was still alive. His head began to clear and his aim steadied. Carter lowered his weapon, what was left of his face was mashed into an expression of acceptance and failure.

Danny had won.

By the time the shot had risen to echo across the harbour, Carter's body had crumpled into a broken mess. It hit the floor with a thud as Danny slowly lowered the weapon. As he watched the blood spreading out almost lazily to stain the stone masonry, he promised himself that now, it was finally over.

"Checkmate," he muttered to himself.

Danny threw the weapon to the ground and then turned away from the body of his enemy and strode towards the stairs without a backwards glance.

Epilogue

Dominion

It felt like the clock had already begun to tick my life away, like sands draining through an hour glass until nothing remained.

Carter was dead and I was alive. It was the only victory I would ever claim.

I had been foolish to believe that Carter's death would somehow stop whatever The Rogues had planned for this country, but all it did was start a chain reaction that would one day lead me to one thing . . .

I looked into the eyes of the men in front of me as they prepared to strike. And there was nothing I could do to stop it.

I remembered back to the events of the past day, and to my discovery that they were planning an attack on London. I don't know why I even reacted when I retrieved the phone from Carter's body.

At the time I was thankful that Jack had met me half way and we'd sped across country in a half-crazed attempt to stop the attack, whatever it was. In a city this big, you can hide pretty easily, even more so when the enemy was one you couldn't see. We had probed the capital, until it led us to Trafalgar Square itself.

Of course it was packed, packed to the brim with tourists and the many other nameless innocents who had been caught up in the hellish combat that preceded a crusade against the dominion itself. I was battle weary, but alert, and when the strike began I was the only person who had noticed it. As the sound of gunfire filled the air around us, I knew that there never had been any stopping it and I had been an idiot to believe otherwise. We tried to find cover as hell seemed to appear in front of us, and that was when Jack fell.

A lone man twenty metres off to his left had suddenly rushed him, and I caught just the faintest glint of silver as he plunged the knife into his chest. Jack collapsed to the floor as death took him for his own, and his killer turned to look very deliberately at me with an accusing stare that I could never forget. He turned to run, and I tore after him, such was the anger that I felt.

Through alleys and narrow streets we raced. I had nothing but rage to force me on; nothing on this earth would stop me now.

I only recognised the sound of the explosion as I was blasted off of my feet. Rubble and bits of timber and masonry landed all around me as I hit the floor. And then everything went black.

Lightning Source UK Ltd.
Milton Keynes UK
UKOW052258270412

191646UK00001B/21/P